DON'T LOOK BACK, JACK!

DON'T LOOK BACK, JACK!

Scottish Traveller Tales

Duncan Williamson

CANONGATE

First published in 1990
by Canongate Publishing Limited
16 Frederick Street, Edinburgh

British Library Cataloguing in Publication Data
Williamson, Duncan 1928–
Don't look back, Jack! : Scottish traveller tales.
I. Title
823.914 [F]
ISBN 0-86241-309-5

Typeset by Hewer Text Composition Services, Edinburgh
Printed and bound in Great Britain
by Billing & Sons, Worcester

to Taffy,
the little cobblestone maker

CONTENTS

EDITOR'S NOTE

During the past eight years Duncan Williamson has published and broadcast, in books, journals, on television and radio a hundred folk tales, a tiny fraction of the thousands he knows. Recently he has been hailed in Exeter and Tyneside as 'the greatest living English-speaking storyteller'. But the first story Duncan Williamson ever recorded for a folklorist was a tale about Jack the common lad and son of a widow, who saved the kingdom from an evil giant by his honesty, candour and kind heartedness. The time of this recording was the summer of 1976, and the folklorist was myself, also Duncan's wife. Duncan, like other fine tradition bearers of his people, took great pleasure in recording for interested students the versions of folk tales he had heard, learned and told from childhood.

Dr Alan Bruford of the School of Scottish Studies encouraged us to continue recording on tape Duncan's repertoire of stories. I began making a card catalogue with summaries of all the tales Duncan would recall which we did not have time to record in the evenings. By the summer of 1980 I had catalogued more than three hundred traditional stories, with sixty centred around a protagonist called Jack. By the spring of 1990 Duncan had recalled a total of eighty 'Jack tales'.

These stories are not compositions of Duncan's. They are tales of heroes, fools, tricksters, elves, speaking animals, wizards, kings and henwives which Duncan came to know by an exceptional aural memory of storytellers he had met during fifty years of travelling the West and North Highlands, the North-East, South and Central Scotland and Fife. The most important feature of a folk tale is not its unique beauty or originality, but the comparative themes and motifs linking it to similar versions of the story told around the world in widely differing cultures by people of disparate ethnic backgrounds. There are interesting parallels that can be drawn between the folk tales of the Nordic, Celtic and Ural-Altaic nations and Duncan Williamson's Jack tales. But for the purposes of this book we consider the stories about Jack to be the most exciting, primordial and wonderful tales of the Scottish oral tradition.

The language of the forty Jack tales Duncan Williamson has recorded to date is a rich strain of Scottish English, displaying great versatility in style and flexibility in the use of Scots idioms. A narration can be more or less Scots depending upon several factors. The primary influence is from whom Duncan has heard a particular story version; his source. For example, if an Aberdeenshire traveller first told Duncan the story, then Duncan is most likely to imitate the North-East dialect in dialogues between characters (re 'Jack and the Potter's Gift'). Another influence on dialectal degree in narration is the audience of listeners who give feedback to the story-teller. For example, in 'The Princess' Pearls', Duncan told the story to traveller relatives who enjoyed familiar details expressly and so his style was more colloquial. A third factor is Duncan's awareness of a particular intended audience in recording sessions. For example, the American students of the Appalachian Centre in Tennessee were very much in Duncan's thoughts when he told 'The Wee Ball of Thread', so the speech was more English. In my editing I have not attempted to standardise spellings from story to story, rather I have tried to mirror the storyteller's linguistic fluidity.

The twelve stories in this collection were chosen from two recording periods, 1976 to 1979 and 1989 to 1990. 'The Golden Boat', 'Three Drunken Elves', 'The Princess' Pearls' and 'The Pots' were recorded in the late 1970s when Duncan and I were still living year round in the traditional 'gelly', a traveller-made bow tent of tree saplings covered with canvas. Travellers were continuously visiting us and storytelling was a very natural, everyday occurrence. 'The Black Thief of Slane', 'The Factor', 'Potter's Gift' and 'Jack's Dream' were recorded in 1989 on the Isle of Skye, and in 1990 in the Black Isle and the Isle of Lewis. Travel to the Highlands and Islands for hero tale research was made possible by grants from the Carnegie Trust, the Centre for Appalachian Studies (East Tennessee State University), the Society of Authors and the Scottish Arts Council. Storytelling sessions on these trips were planned in advance and were given for native Gaelic speakers or for our research assistants. The balance of stories were recorded in the spring of 1990 for family, friends and fellow storytellers coming to ceilidh at our fireside in Lizziewells farmhouse, Fife. These were very relaxed sessions and 'I Found a Thing', 'Wee Ball of Thread', 'Beggar's Island' and 'Farmer's Treasure' have great magical force.

The twelve stories in this collection are published here complete for the first time. All have been transcribed virtually verbatim from taped recordings now lodged in the School of Scottish Studies, Edinburgh University. I wish to thank the senior technician of the School, Mr Fred Kent, for his patience in making the copies for my transcription and for the Appalachian Centre. I also wish to thank the grant awarding bodies mentioned above for their financial and professional support.

Linda Williamson
Collessie, Fife, 1990

JACK

After fifty years of collecting folk tales through many parts of Scotland, the character who comes most important is Jack. Now people has asked me, 'Who is Jack?' And why is he so important in other countries? For you have Jack in Germany and Russia and in America, in Canada. In France and Holland, even in Africa and in China; though he may have a different name there the tales about him are the same. But Jack was not one particular person. In the tales Jack takes many forms. He is a piece of everyman. The reason you've got Jack all over the world is because people needed, for their storytelling they needed a hero. This hero could be a fool, he could be clever, he could be big, he could be strong. But in every individual story Jack is a different person. He was just a person's hero, built from a construction of storytellers. Now in my collection of stories I have Jack being a slave, I have Jack being a woodcutter, Jack a beachcomber, Jack a fool, Jack the trickster, Jack the hero. Because everybody had their own idea who Jack was.

Jack to the travellers was a local folk hero. And to be a folk hero he had to be a certain kind o' person. Storytellers built him up to be this certain kind o' person and they wanted to keep him that way. With only one exception, and I have collected at least a couple o' hundred stories about Jack in my travels, Jack is never old. Also with one exception Jack is never a child. He is almost always either a young teenager or a young man. And he was never the older brother, always the younger. If there were three brothers in the story, one of them had to be Jack, and Jack was always the youngest. The youngest brother was always the hero! Jack never had any sisters. And Jack may have ended up married, but you don't get anything about the marriage. Or he may have ended up in the lion's mouth or the dragon's mouth, but he always escapes. In my tradition Jack never dies. And he's always welcome with the king, he's the king's favourite! Sometimes he's lazy, sometimes he's foolish. But when it comes to the crunch of the story Jack's not as foolish as folk think he is! And Jack was never feart. Jack was always brave. Oh, he was well known by the women, and loved by some of them! In the stories Jack was always handsome and good looking, even though he lay by the fire and grew a beard and never washed hissel. Apart from one story where Jack's father is an old seaman with a peg-leg, his father is usually not present. He lives with his mother. But why is his mother always important? And why do we not hear about Jack's father or about Jack's sisters? Look to the stories!

Why they called him 'Jack' I don't know. Why not Tom, Dick, Harry or Peter? Even in the Bible you don't have a Jack. Well, there are many jacks in this world; a boot jack, car jack, jack knife, you can name hundreds and hundreds. There's a steeple jack and a jack stone—just think how many jacks you could get! And all these jacks have something in common with each other: they are all useful in our everyday work. I believe a few hundred years ago that Jack was a very popular name, although today it is more usually John or Iain in Scotland. In traveller society, fathers always called one of their sons Jack, you had a Jack or John in every family.

Where did Jack come from? I can't explain this because I don't know. Who built and constructed all these wonderful stories about Jack no one can ever tell. I can only tell you a few stories, and then you build your own picture. You see, some of these stories about Jack go back a long long time. And in a lot of them much was left to your own idea. The storytellers didna make it as plain to you like a children's schoolbook. Everything wasna laid out to you. Like dream stories, it's always been a mystery!

I FOUND A THING, I FOUND A THING!

In early spring, March and April, when the travellers begint to go on their move, old Sandy Reid came on a visit to Argyllshire with his pony and his cart and his family. He was my mother's brother-in-law. When he put his tent by the shoreside, the first thing us kids would do—livin in the Furnace wood all winter by wirsels without ony visitors—we'd rush doon. And Aunt Belloch would make us tea, she would gie us a tin jug o' tea, and say, 'Come on, weans, Uncle Sandy's going to tell us a story!' She loved stories too, God rest her soul. And it was a good get-together. They came every year from Dumbarton to see us. And this is one of the many, many wonderful stories he would tell us in cant and traveller style.

Jack and his two brothers lived with their mother in a small cottage away out in the forest, because Jack's father had been a woodcutter. And he had died for some reason, maybe through drink, maybe through an accident, it's hard to tell. We don't have very much about his father, but the story brings ye to his brothers, his two older brothers. There werena much between them, maybe a couple o' year or so. Jack was the youngest. The two brothers worked in the wood. But when they went off to work they had a problem, and their problem was Jack. Jack was lazy.

They coaxed him every morning, 'Look, Jack, we have to feed you, we have to take care of you. Could you no come and give us a wee help in the wood?'

1

An' Jack would lie by the fire waitin for his brothers to bring back the logs from the wood on their backs. Jack would put them on the fire. He wouldnae wash, he wouldnae shave, he wouldnae keep hissel tidy. He wore the same old coat day out and day in. And his brothers got kind o' fed up with their younger brother Jack. The thing was, the two older brothers were big, tall, handsome young men, but Jack was the most handsome of them all! Even though he lay by the fireside an' he grew a beard. And the same old coat, an' the dust and ashes fell on him.

He would lie there an' his mother would say, 'Jack, do ye want a cup o' tea?'

He would say, 'Well, give it doon here tae me.' Jack was lazy, completely lazy.

And because he was lazy his brothers would say, 'Och, let's forget about him. He's too stupid. He'll never come to nothing!'

So the two brothers continued to work and bring in the money to their mother from the cutting of the timber in the wood. And helped to support Jack as he lay by the fireside. Now every Saturday afternoon after the hard day's work, the brothers would go to the town and have a glass o' beer or a drink in the village. But Jack was not allowed to come. Jack never got money, because Jack never worked for any money. But the mother herself she loved Jack from all her heart. She knew he was lazy, she knew he would never come to nothing, he was a good-for-nothing. Anyhow, he was still her son. And she respected Jack. When the two brothers were gone to work, Jack lay by the fireside with the ashes fallin over him and his beard hangin doon—not a grey beard, but a beautiful, beautiful blonde beard. And beautiful blonde hair hangin down his back—Jack was a beautiful young man. He never knew it, but his mother knew. And because he had beautiful blonde hair and blue eyes and he was the youngest of the family, his mother loved him dearly.

She would make excuses to his older brothers, 'Och, it's

2

just yir wee brother an' he's no at hissel. He's no richt, ye ken.'

His brothers would say, 'Well, he's big and strong, as good as us. He could come and give us a wee help.'

'Och, jist leave him alane, laddie,' she said. 'Dinnae bother him, he's jist yir poor wee brother.'

But this went on for a long, long time. And Jack grew up till he was the age of twenty-one. And one afternoon the two brothers went to the town as usual. But when they cam back, they were excited. Oh, they had a little drink of course, but they were over the moon.

And Mother could see they were so excited. She said, 'What happened, boys, what's all the excitement about?'

'Oh, Mother,' he said, 'ye've nae idea. There's couriers gaun roond the village cryin out that the princess in the town, the neighbouring big town has sent out a challenge to all the young men—that the only man she'll ever marry can answer three questions. And tomorrow is a special day. People are comin from all over the countryside. And the princess is gaunna sit there in her big garden in front o' the palace, invitin all the young men from around the countryside to come. The one that can answer three questions for her she will marry. But no one else.'

But the mother says, 'Boys, what are ye gaunnae dae aboot it?'

'Oh, Mother,' he said, 'we're gaun the morn! The morn's the first day an' we're gaun!'

Oh well, the old mother was awfa pleased aboot it, ye see. Noo, Jack, he's lyin by the fireside. And he's listenin to aa this. He's lyin stretched oot at the front o' the fire, it was a big old open fire, burnin logs. And he's listenin. But he never said a word.

So that night they all went off to their beds. But Jack always slept by the fireside. He never went to any bed. So the next morning the two brothers cam doon, Tommy and Willie.

3

And Jack said, 'Tommy and Willie, whaur are ye gaun?'

They said, 'What dae ye mean, whaur are we gaun? We're gaun to the toon, the big toon. Today is the big day. And we've got tae compete against knights and noblemen and everybody. The princess has asked everybody tae come, we're included. We're human beings, we're gaun.'

And Jack said, 'I'm gaun tae.'

'What!' Thomas said, 'what did you say?'

He said, 'I'm gaun wi yese.'

'No, Jack, ye're no gaun wi us,' they said. 'You're not included. We're gaun by wirsel.'

But the mother she made them a big pot o' porridge and goat's milk and they had a good breakfast. The boys tidied theirsels up and shaved and washed and put on their best clothes that they had. And off they set, to walk to the village and to the town. It was about four miles to the big town where there was the palace o' the princess. So the boys said good-bye to their mother, and from where they lived in the forest they had to travel a long narrow twisted road till they came to the village.

Jack was still lyin by the fire wi the ashes comin fae the lum faain on him, soot faain on him. His coat was burnt in bits wi sparks faain on it. Sparks faain on his hair, some o' his hair, his beautiful long blonde hair was burnt wi sparks faain. But Jack never minded. He used to gie hissel a shake when the sparks fell on him, that was aa that happened. After the two brothers Tommy and Willie had walked oot Jack got up.

He says, 'Mother, I'm gaun tae!'

She says, 'Jack, no, son, dinnae gang wi them.'

He says, 'What do ye mean, Mother? I'm a human being tae.'

'Jack, laddie,' she said, 'look, mammy'll mak ye a bonnie cup o' tea an' I'll make ye a scone, I'll make ye a bannock, I'll mak ye onything. Dinnae bother, brother! These laddies'll get into trouble afore the end o' the thing happens.

4

And I dinnae want you to get into trouble. You're my wean!'

'Mother,' he says, 'I'm gaun! I'm gaun tae, I'll follae them.'

She says, 'Look, if you follae them, they'll kill ye, they'll gie ye a beatin! They'll beat you up.'

'I'm no heedin,' he said, 'I'm gaun.'

So he had his breakfast and never washed his face. He gaed oot the door and he gied hissel a shake. The dust and ashes flew aff him, it blackened the whole hoose for about half an hour. And on he went doon the road.

So Tommy and Willie they're walkin on. Something happened to Tommy, but he said, 'This is a lang road, brother, but we'll no be long, we'll hurry on.' He glanced his eye back the way they'd come. And he looked and he saw Jack. He said, 'Willie, look what's comin behind us!'

'What do ye mean, what's comin behind us?'

He said, 'Look, Jack's after us. Jack's comin.'

'Oh no, brother,' he said, 'Jack cannae come! He'll shame us, he'll put us to shame. We'll get the jail if he comes wi us. We'll stop, wait till he comes, we'll tell him.'

So Jack hurried on, travelled doon the path. Two brothers is waiting. Jack comes.

Willie says, 'Where do ye think ye're gaun?'

He said, 'I'm gaun wi yese.'

'No, you're no,' he said, 'you're no gaun wi us. Look, go back afore we're gaunnae kill ye deid! Or gie ye a beatin. We're gaunnae kill ye, if ye don't go back!'

Jack said, 'I'm gaun wi yese.'

So the two brothers catcht him, one on each side. And they flung him into a ditch—tae the neck in water tae there. 'Now,' he says, 'go back to yir mother!'

So they travelled on. On and on they travelled and it was Willie this time, he looked back. Here was Jack comin again, toddlin after them, him all soakin wet, his beard soakin wet, his hair soakin wet, his claes soakin wet, full o' gutters and

5

muck fae the drain tae there! He said, 'He's comin again! Well, if he's comin again, he's gaunna get it this time!'

And then Jack stopped. For lyin beside the road was a bit crooked stick. A crooked stick, it looked like a stave. And Jack picked it up and he said, 'I found a thing, I found a thing and youse dinna ken what it is!'

And the two brothers said, 'We'd better wait tae see what he's got.'

So Jack walked up with this crooked stick. He said, 'I found a thing, I found a thing.'

'Jack, it's only a bit stick ye're haudin. Whaur do ye think ye're gaun?' So they started and they gied him another beatin. They flung him in the ditch again. But Jack still held his stick. So on they went again. But they hadna gone far doon another turn in the main road gaun to the village, when here comes Jack toddlin after them again!

Tommy looked roond his shouder, he said, 'Brother, he's still comin again. Look, we cannae go to the village—we'll have to gae hame wi him.'

Willie says, 'No, I'm no gaun hame wi him. I'm gaunnae kill him this time when he comes up. I'm gaunnae kill him deid!'

But just before he cam up to the brothers, what was lyin on the roadside, it dropped from a wagon or a horse wagon, but a big tattie! A big tattie fell to the roadside. And Jack picked it up. He looked at it, 'I found a thing, I found a thing, you dinnae ken what it is, oh! Ye're no gaunnae get it!'

They thought it was something special. So they waited till he cam up and he opened his hand . . . a big tattie. 'Are ye gaun home, Jack, or are we gaunna kill ye? Ye cannae come wi us!'

· He says, 'I found a thing, I found a thing, youse dinnae ken what it is and you're no gaunnae get it!'

They looked, a big tattie lyin green by the roadside. They gied him another beatin again, they flung him in another ditch. And they walked on. He said, 'That'll maybe fix him this time!'

So Jack lay there for a few minutes. The two brothers travelled on. Lo and behold they hadna gone far, but Jack got up oot o' the ditch. He's soakin wet again. He put the big tattie in his pocket, he said, 'It'll come in handy.' So he travelled on and he travelled on again.

And Willie looked ower his shouder again, he said, 'He's comin again, brother, he's comin again! He's gaunnae shame us. We cannae gang, look, we'll have to tak him hame. We'll have to kill him deid, we'll have to murder him! I'll choke him black in the face!'

He said, 'Willie, brother, ye cannae choke him black in the face!'

'I'll choke him,' he said, 'I'll kill him, this time he's dead.' But when they cam up through the end of the wood there was a wee green field. And the front of the field was full o' mole-hills, ye ken the way the moles dig up. Willie says, 'This is where I end his days. He's no gaun another step. He's finished!' So they stopped and when Jack cam up, he said, 'Jack, whaur do ye think ye're gaun?'

He said, 'I tellt ye I'm gaun wi ye!'

'No ye're no!' So the two brothers dived on him. And they got him doon. And they covered him. He had an auld hat on his heid. And they took all the molehills, they filled the hat-full o' sand and they put it on his heid. And they beat him up, they covered him with sand and left him there. 'That'll finish him. Now, maybe he'll learn a lesson, maybe he'll go back tae his mother!' So the two boys by this time had only a step to the village and on they travelled, on their journey.

Jack he got up again. His pockets were full o' sand, his neck was full o' sand, his old hat was full of sand. He pulled the hat on his heid. Even his wee crooked stick was covered wi sand! Wi the molehills. He said, 'Wherever they're gaun, I'm gaun!' But he kept well behind them this time. He travelled through the village on to the main track, and the boys disappeared in

7

the crowd. Because they cam at last to the palace. There was the big palace o' the princess sittin on the hill, and there were all the people. Knights on white horses and farmers dressed in their best.

Now there was a beautiful garden leadin to the palace. And a big gate, and the gate was flung open. There were guards on each side of the palace. And there sat the princess on a beautiful throne inside the garden. With two guards by her side. And all the people from the palace standin by her side. One by one everybody cam in. Only one person was allowed in at a time. Knights left their horses, jumped off and some in coats of armour. Some dressed like . . . nobody could explain the way they were dressed. They appeared before the princess.

So it was a beautiful sunny day, but Jack he stood an' waited with his crooked stick in his hand, his tattie in his pocket, his hat full o' sand—he never even took the sand oot his hat! His wee crooked stick was full o' sand where the two brothers had near buried him in the molehills. And there he stood. The sun was high in the sky and the young princess sat there, beautiful young princess, red hair. An' three questions she would give to you.

She said, 'A fire in the hearth?'

And the knight stood there. He said, 'A fire in the hearth?' They hadn't a clue.

'Take him away!'

Next one came. 'Fire in my hearth?' she asked. Next one. 'Take him away! Fire in the hearth? . . . Take him away.'

One by one. Now the sun was climbin over the sky, as one by one no one could answer the question. Tommy cam, before the princess, bowed before the princess.

'Oh,' she says, 'young man, you've come to answer my question.' Because Tommy was a good lookin boy. 'Fire in the hearth?'

He stood dumb.

'Take him away.'

8

So one by one they went and one by one they went, until there was only one person left standin at the gate. In rags, a coat burnt with the sparks from the fire, hair burnt wi the sparks from the fire. Long blonde hair hangin doon his back and the blonde hair and two blue eyes and a black dirty face covered with sand and a crooked stick. And the guard said, 'Well, my lady that's everyone.' And no one has answered the questions.

Tommy and Willie were so upset, they couldna answer the princess' question. They'd lost Jack in the crowd and passed by and never saw him. They were so broken-hearted. They walked home wishin to their heart they would never see Jack again. For they thought they had buried him in the mole heaps. They said, 'If he's still alive we'll pick him up on the road back. We'll drag him oot to my mother.'

So the princess said, 'Is that everyone then? Is no one going to answer my questions? Is there no one left?'

And one of the guards said, 'My lady, there is a beggarman at the gate.'

'A beggarman?' she said. 'What do you mean, a beggarman?'

'Well, my majesty, my highness, he looks like a beggarman.'

'Well,' she said, 'he's a human being, he's one of my subjects—bring him before me!'

The last person was Jack. And they brought him up and he stood with his coat burnt and his beautiful blonde beard burnt with sparks, an' his long blonde hair burnt with sparks covered in muck and sand. And they had buried him in the mole heap wi a crooked stick in his hand. And the princess looked and she saw the two beautiful blue eyes and the fair eyebrows. She knew this was a young man. This was a young man who had been neglected. And she could see through all the dirt.

She says, 'Young man, where have you come from?'

He said, 'I cam from the wood from my mother!'

9

She says, 'Do you think you could come and answer my questions?'

'Well,' he said, 'I've come to try!'

She said, 'There's a fire in the hearth?'

And Jack said, 'I've a tattie, let us cook it!'

Princess smiles. She said, 'We could burn wir fingers?'

He said, 'I've got a stick!'

She said, 'It's all dirty?'

He said, 'I've got a hatful.'

Princess clapped her hands, the princess clapped her hands! She says, 'This is him, this is the one I want. It's over.'

Jack was rushed away. Into the palace. All the footmen carried him off by foot and hand and head into a great bath —put him in, shaved him, washed him, dressed him, cleaned him! Got him all the most beautiful clothes. The princess was still waiting in her chamber.

'Go bring the man,' she said, 'now to me after you've cleaned him up!' And Jack was brought before her. Hair clipped short. Beard gone. Brand new clothes. Washed and polished. There stood the most beautiful man she'd ever saw in all her life. And immediately the princess fell in love with him. 'Oh my darling,' she said, 'you have answered my questions. And now,' she said, 'the're going to be a wedding!'

But anyhow, sad Tommy and Willie wandered home back through the town. Back through the village, searched the mole heaps for Jack. But Jack was gone. 'Whaur do ye think he went?' he said. 'That silly brother o' wirs.'

'Oh,' he said, 'let's hope he never went to the palace. Look, if he's gotten in the palace in front o' the princess, we'll all be arrested, we'll be sent to jail.' They couldna find him, so they went home to their mother. Oh, their mother had their tea waitin for them.

She said, 'Boys, did ye see Jack?'

'Mother,' he said, 'look, what do ye mean, did we see Jack? He followed us to the toon. We beat him. We tried to send him back . . . has he come hame?'

10

'No,' she said. 'Laddies, what hae ye done to yir wee brother? Ye ken he's yir ain wee brother!'

'Well, Mother,' he said, 'look, if he goes to the toon in that state and goes to the palace, look, he's gaunna get us all arrested. Look, we're gaunna be jailed if he goes before the princess in that state he is!'

So they waited for two days. They waited for three days, for four days. But still Jack never cam back. But meantime, what they didn't know was the're a large wedding goin on! Jack was gettin married to the princess. And for five days they waited. Still Jack never cam back.

And Tommy says to his brother, 'Maybe we killt him, brother. Mebbe he's deid. Maybe we beat him too much.' And they felt a little sad for Jack. 'After all,' says Tommy, 'it was wir wee brother, we shouldna been sae hard on him.'

'But if he'd only washed hissel and tidied hissel up and helped us in the wood, look, it would be different,' says Willie.

'Well anyway,' he said, 'he's gone noo anyway.'

And the old mother was broken-hearted. She said, 'What have you done to my wean?'

And they tellt her. They gaed up and tellt her, 'Mother,' he said, 'he followed us. We beat him, look, we gied him a beatin. We never hurtit him, but we gied him a beatin. Three times we beat him and three times we sent him back. And then we buried him in the mole heaps in the field. But he still wouldna go back.'

'Well,' she said, 'there's only one thing. He must hae went to the toon. And he must hae went to the palace. And he got hissel arrested, and he's got thrown in the dungeons.'

'Oh, Mother,' he said, 'what's gaunna happen?'

They were still discussin what was gaunna happen after five days had passed. They never went to work. Noo, there's a big drive leadin up to the wee hoose in the forest where they lived. But unknown to them, the princess had married and

11

fallen in love with Jack. They'd had a great party together. They had wined and dined for three long days.

And she said, 'Jack, do you have any family?'

He said, 'Yes, my darling, I have some family. I have two brothers and my mother.'

'Well,' she said, 'look, she's my mother-in-law, and these are my brothers-in-law.' And now after Jack had married her and slept three nights with her, she said, 'Wouldn't it be nice if you would take me to visit your people, visit your mother and your brothers? I would love to see them.' So a great coach was laid on for the princess and her husband. They were to go for a drive, for the first time after the wedding.

And Jack said to the coachman, 'Just drive on! And I'll give ye directions!' He was a young bene cowl dressed with his hair all combed and tidied, the most beautiful young man you ever saw, just like yourself. Dressed in all these beautiful clothes the princess had provided for him, because the princess was really in love with him. And he drove on through the big town, down through the village, up the long driveway that led to Jack's house.

But at that very moment Tommy and Willie said, 'Mother, look, we cannae go on any longer. Something's happened tae him, we'll have to go to the village and look for him.' When then they spied the coach coming up. Two white horses, a footman sitting. And a young lady and gentleman sitting on the coach, a beautiful coach.

Oh, the old woman cam up, she put her hand in front of her eyes an' she deeked out, with the sun, ye see. She says, 'Bene hantle bingin, brothers. They're bene hantle bingin.' Oh, Willie and Tommy stood there by their mother's side. The coach pulled up in front o' the house. And the young gentleman stepped out. And he opened the door, he put his hand out and then the young lady stepped out. Dressed in a white dress. 'Shanness, shanness,' says the old mort, 'bene hantle! What is the bene hantle daein here?'

He said, 'I tellt ye, naismort. It's that silly brother o' wirs.

This is the bene mort he got in trouble. This is the bene mort got in trouble noo! Oh, we're fir the quod! We're gaun to the quod. That's the silly mental brother o' wirs got us in trouble.'

So the two young people walked up to where the old woman was standing. And he turned round and he said, 'My darling, this is my mother.'

And the old woman stood in amazement! And she recognised the blue eyes. But she didnae understand who it was.

He says, 'Mother, do you not recognise me? Do you not know me, Mother?'

She says, 'Gentleman, who are you? You look familiar to me, I've saw you before.'

He says, 'Mammy, Mother, I'm Jack!'

Tommy and Willie stood there in amazement.

And the young princess said, 'Now introduce me to your mother and to your two brothers.'

So Jack said, 'My darling, this is my mother, and this is my brother Tommy and my brother Willie. And they live here in the forest, and they were the cause of me comin to see you in the first place.'

And she said, 'My dear, this is not much of a home for to have your old mother stay in. Can't we bring your family home with you to the palace?'

And Jack said, 'It will be very very nice to have my mother home with me to the palace. But not those two! Let me take my mother home with me, my darling. But let these two stay here for the rest of their lives. And remember how they beat me up and wouldn't take me with them the day I went to meet you!'

'All right, my dear,' says the princess.

And the old woman jumped in the coach and off she went back to the palace wi her son Jack and the princess. And as for Willie and Tommy, they stayed in that old hoose till they were old men, till the hoose fell atop o' them! And Jack never went to see them again. He lived a very happy life with his mother and his princess. And that's the end of my story.

JACK AND THE GOLDEN BOAT

I remember I was about seventeen, and I came one night to old Johnnie MacDonald's camping place just outside o' Coupar Angus. And he was a great storyteller. And I wanted a story. I'd be a young man—I should have been away courting a woman or something—I wasna interested in that! I loved to listen to stories, to gather knowledge. So I said to old Johnnie, 'Johnnie, I want you to tell me a story!' He said, 'If you want me to gie you a story, would ye get me a wee bit tobacco?' He smoked a pipe, you see. You know, I walked four mile from Wolf Hill to Coupar Angus for a half an ounce o' tobacco and I walked back, for one story on a night of heavy snow! That's the God's honest truth. When I came back old Johnnie MacDonald sat with me, and this is what he told me that night.

Jack lived with his mother in a little cottage by the sea. And Jack's father had been a beachcomber—he had spent his entire life searchin the beach for anything; flotsam and jetsam that was cast in by the sea. But Jack at that time was only a boy. When Jack's father died, the only thing he left Jack's mother was two pigs—a boar and a sow. While Jack was still a boy the old boar died. But his mother was left with the old sow. And that was all that Jack's mother had. Every day Jack had to go and feed this sow, and Jack hated this job. From his entire life, he hated feedin this old pig. He detested the pig! Because he had to feed it every morning.

14

But one morning the old mother says to Jack, 'Jack, you'd better be very careful this morning because the auld sow last night had some piglets.' Where the old mother got the sow covered I don't know. But it had seven piglets. And she says, 'Jack, I want you to be very special careful tae look after these seven piglets, and see that nothing happens to them!'

To keep his old mother pleased, he went down one morning and he looked and he fed the sow. One o' the wee piglets was tangled up among the straw. And Jack hated the mother and everything attached to pigs! But he felt a wee bit sad for this wee piglet, it was the youngest. He wandered up and it was tied among the straw in the pigsty, fankled and it couldna get movin. Jack took it and he picked it up in his arms, and he held it in his hands. It wasna very big. 'My wee cratur,' he said, 'I dinnae like yir mother or I dinnae like aa yir family. But to see you stranglet among the straw, I couldna take it. Yir mother is only fit for human meat! And aa yir brothers and sisters is nae good. But you my wee piglet, I wouldna see you chokit among the straw. I'll take ye and I'll pit ye in beside yir mother.' So Jack took the wee piglet and he put it aside its mother.

He walked up to his mother and his mother gied him a wee taste o' something to eat. And it was a bonnie beautiful day. He was bidin by the sea. 'Ach,' he says, 'Mother, I think I'll go for a walk away alang the shore and gather some driftwood.' So away goes Jack and he travels on and he travels on along the shore. Now the sun was scorchin, a beautiful day.

But he wandered about four or five mile along the shore when all in a moment he thought he would sit doon. The sun was scorchin high in the heavens. He sat doon beside this big rock. And he was worried, he says, 'Why is it I should have to feed my mother's pigs, that's aa I ever dae. Pig this, pig that, pig this and pig that, pig this, feed the pig, feed the pig, Jack, feed the pig, Jack, go doon and look after the pig, Jack—I never dae anything except look after my mother's pig. That's all I dae—I'm no event as good as a pig! My mother disna even class me as good as a pig. She thinks more o' the pigs than me!'

But the sun was risin over the water, and Jack's lyin back beside this big rock in the shade. And he looks oot across the water, he sees something comin in floatin with the tide. It was the very drollest thing he'd ever seen in his life . . . it looked like a boat. But he couldna distinguish if it was a boat or not, you see. But it was comin closer and closer and closer and closer. But it was shinin like gold! Shinin like gold. And Jack lay back against the rock. 'Well, I'm gaunna watch what this thing,' he says . . . 'I know my father, who was a beachcomber many years ago, had got many things comin in with the tide. Maybe this is something special.' Jack lays back against the rock and he watched and he watched and he watched it. And in it cam closer and closer and closer. And the tide was comin in, and comin in and comin in. And when it cam in closer, sure enough the thing was a boat! A beautiful, beautiful golden boat.

And Jack rubbed his hands thegither, 'It's a boat,' he said. 'All my life I would like to have a sail; I never had a sail in a boat,' he said. 'But I'm goin to in this boat!' And the boat cam in with the tide. And Jack stepped in, and the minute he stepped in the boat, the boat turned around. Away it set off. And Jack was sailin beautiful over the waves like that. And sure enough with the sailin in the waves Jack fell sound asleep in the beautiful boat. He was relaxed, he was contented for evermore. He was in this boat and he was sailin in the sea.

But lo and behold he had sailed on and sailed on, all in a minute the boat landed in another land, on earth, on a beach. Jack rubbed his eyes. 'God bless my soul and body, what happened to me?' he said. 'Am I dreamin or am I asleep or what am I thinkin on? But I must hae had a hurl in a boat,' he said. And he lookit roon, there was the boat. There was the golden boat, the most beautiful golden boat he ever saw in his life. And he lookit round, he seen

16

this bonnie island and palm trees and everything. And this
beautiful path leading up.

'Well,' he says, 'the boat took me here and I'm gaun tae
see where it took me tae.' And he stepped up the path, he
walkit up, and the minute he walked up the path he hadna
gone two hundred yards when the first thing cam doon meetin
him was a pig! And seven pigs after her, seven young pigs. But
the funny thing about thes pigs, they didna walk on four feet,
they walked on two feet! And this pig had a crown on her
heid and she had this long flowin dress, and all these wee
pigs comin behind her each dressed in a beautiful dress.

And she said, 'Halt!' Jack stopped. 'Why do you come to
our land?' she says. 'Why are you invadin our land? You
human, why do you come here?'

Jack said, 'I'm sorry, excuse me, I'm a wee bit baffled,
I'm a wee bit mixed up.' He said, 'I cam in a boat.'

'Well,' she shouted back, 'guards come here!' And afore
you could say another word Jack was surrounded by about
fifteen pigmen with spears and helmets on them walkin up
behind him. She says, 'Take him and throw him in the
dungeons. He's only fit for pigmeat.'

Jack was arrested, to be flung in the dungeons. Noo he
didna ken what in the world was gaun wrong. He was
mesmerised and stupefied. He didna ken what was wrong.
He was took, marched back hand and fit to the castle, thrown
in the dungeons and he lay for hours. And he didna ken what
was wrong. Then all in a minute, out comes the guard and
the gate was opened and he was marched up! In front o'
the throne, in front o' the queen! And there the queen was
sittin—a pig! Sittin in her robes and silvery robes, a crown
on her heid.

She says, 'A mortal being, you are charged for invadin
our land.'

Jack said, 'Yir Majesty, what harm have I done?'

She says, 'You hate pigs of all description. You said "in
your entire life that we were only fit for human meat". Well,'

17

she says, 'you're only fit for pigmeat! You're sentenced to death! And to the dungeons you will go. And tomorrow morning you shall be hung, drawn and quartered and made into pigmeat. Take him away!'

Poor Jack was marched away. Jack looked at the queen, and he looked at all the wee piglets—princesses they were! They werena piglets, they were princesses dressed in robes. But one o' them, the youngest one, she looked and she smiled. They had pigs' feet! But they had hands and they had bodies. But they were only pigs from the bottom doon, they had pigs' feet. And the wee-est ane smiled at Jack and she laughed at Jack. And it made him happy to even see one pig, one friend among the lot. She smiled at Jack and he wasna half sae sad—well, he knew he was sentenced to death. He knew he was finished. He was threwn in the dungeons.

He lay in the dungeons among the wee puckle straw. And he must hae lay for hours and hours and hours. When all in a minute he heard a key click. Click in the lock. And the door opened. And in cam the smallest princess o' the piggery, smallest o' the queen's princesses, the wee-est one o' the lot.

And she said, 'Jack, are ye sleepin?'

'No,' he said, 'dear, I'm no sleeping. How could I sleep in a place like this?'

She says, 'Jack, you ken, my mother has sentenced you to death. And tomorrow morning you'll only be fit for pigs' meat.'

'But,' he says, 'what can I dae?'

'Well,' she says, 'come wi me. Noo, I'm giein ye one chance. And come wi me,' she said. 'You gied me a chance, you gied me a chance a long long time ago, you dinnae ken nothing aboot. I'm gaunna pay my debt to you, Jack,' she said.

'God bless us,' says Jack, 'I dinnae ken if I'm livin or deid or I'm in the doldrums or what I am. But,' he says, 'what can I dae?'

'Look,' she says, 'I'm lettin you go. And take that wee path doon the way you cam, back to the beach. And ye'll find a boat. Jack, get in that boat! *Jump in it, and dinnae move ti ye get to the other side!* But remember one thing,' she says, 'when ye get to the beach—jump oot! Dinnae wait ti the boat stops—jump before it stops. Because otherwise, if ye dinnae dae that, never again will ye ever have another chance.'

So Jack said cheerio to the wee toy piglet, the wee piglet princess. And he sets oot. Noo he was free. And away he runs. He runs doon the path he cam up, back the path, past this big castle, through this big avenue, doon through this land, back to the beach—and there sure enough lay the golden boat. And Jack jumped in the boat and sat doon. And the minute Jack sat in the boat away goes the boat, off and off. But this time Jack didna sleep. He couldna sleep! No way could he sleep.

And the boat carried on straight through the water, straight up ower the waves and doon ower the waves, doon ower the waves. Till all in a moment Jack lookit and he seen this beach, this familiar beach. And he seen a wee hoose in the distance. He says, 'That's my mother's hoose.' And as the boat was comin on the beach Jack jumped oot. He jumped oot! And the water was tae there—to his waist. He waded in and he sat doon upon a rock. And he lookit. The sun passed under a cloud. And the boat turned, and away went the boat . . .

Jack must hae sat for a long long time at the back o' this rock. And oh, he wakened up. He wakened up and he rubbed his eyes. He lookit. 'God bless my soul and body,' he says, 'I must hae fell asleep! That was a funny dream I had, a terrible dream. I had an awfa dream. That's the pig-people! I've never seen pig-people, never in my life. It's a funny story I'll have to tell my mother when I go back.'

And Jack lookit—the tide was oot! Far away oot. The tide was away far from where he sat by the rock. And Jack felt his legs. And he groped his legs. He was soakin to the waist! Right to there, soakin. 'God bless my soul and body,' he said, 'if the tide's oot and I sat here at the back of the rock and I fell asleep and I dreamed, hoo did I get so wet? Hoo have I been so wet? . . . Well,' he said, 'I'll never know.'

But he had gathered two-three sticks for his mother. 'Well,' he says, 'one thing I ken, I'd better take my mother's wee puckle sticks hame.' He'd gathered sticks that had come in with the tide. So he picked up his puckle sticks and he walked hame to his mother. And he had his sticks on his back. His wee croft was right beside the shore. And he flung the sticks beside his mother's cuddy where he used to cut the sticks. And he walked in to his mother. His old mother had the tea on the table.

And she said, 'Jack, are ye back, son? Whaur were you all this time? You've been away a long long while.'

'Mother,' he said, 'I was away gatherin a wee puckle sticks.'

'Well,' she said, 'yir tea's on the table. Jack, afore ye get yir tea will ye gae and feed the pigs?'

'Aye, Mother,' he said, 'I'll gae and feed yir pigs! I'll be glad tae feed yir pigs,' he says. 'Whaur's the meat, and I'll gie them a good feed?'

She says, 'Jack, what's wrong wi you, laddie? Ye never before used to like to feed the pigs.'

'Mother,' he says, 'I'll feed yir pigs. Frae noo on, I'll feed yir pigs and I'll be good to yir pigs.'

The old mother wanted to find out. She says, 'Jack, what happened to ye?'

He says, 'Mother, nothing happened to me. I was only away for a sail in a golden boat.'

And his mother never understood because he never tellt his mother the story. And she never knew. But I'm tellin you the story, and you can make oot in your mind whatever happened! Because I dinnae ken what happened. And that's the last o' my story!

JACK AND THE PRINCESS' PEARLS

My father told me this story years and years ago when I was
a wee boy. He would tell us one bit the one night, and then
maybe tell us the next bit the next night, and then maybe
another bit the next night! He wouldna tell us it all at once.
But we had to work for it. We had to get sticks, get water
and run messages and dae everything before we'd get a bit
o' story. He'd tell us a bit o' story every night—mostly in the
winter. We were never there in the summertime—we were all
away playin and fishin and daein one thing and another. But
mostly in the winter nights when it was dark early, he'd gather
us all roon about him and tell us a story. This is what we call
a 'fairy story' and I hope you like it.

It was Jack and his two brothers and they stayed in this
wee cottage with their old mother, and they had this wee
croft between them. Their father had died and left the three
laddies with their mother—Sandy and Willie and Jack. Jack
was the youngest and the mother liked him the best because
he done everything for her. The other two were awfa lazy
and they wouldna do much. They made a living by cutting
firewood and selling sticks. The mother sellt two-three eggs
and she kept a coo, she sellt milk and things round about
the district.

But ane day she called them in and she said, 'Look, boys,
noo yese is begin to come young men. And it's about time ye
were tryin tae do something for yirsels, because ye ken I'm

gettin kind of up in years noo and I'm no able to work for ye—if two o' yese would gang and look for a job tae yirsel, go for a wander through the country and ye might get a job and meet a wife and get married—and dinna be a burden to yir auld mither! Because I'm just gettin as much wi my wee puckle eggs and my wee drop milk tae keep mysel gaun.'

So they sat round the house one night and they talked it over. 'Noo,' she says, 'look if yese is gaun the morn dinnae take Jack wi yese.' Jack was the youngest, she thocht the worl o' him.

So they sat talkin late into the early hours o' the morning. Sandy was the oldest, 'Ach,' he says, 'I've made up my mind. I think I'll pack up tomorrow and gae away into the worl, see if I can pitch my fortune and dae whatever I can.'

Willie says, 'I'll go wi ye.'

'Well,' Jack said, 'if yese two 's gaun, there's nae much sense o' me stayin. You'll need someone to look after yese, because I'll tell ye one thing, yese two'll get into trouble if I'm no wi yese.'

They said, 'We can watch wirsel, we dinnae need the likes o' you, a young lad wi us, we can watch wirsel.'

Well, the mother coaxed the lad Jack not to gang. 'Ach, Mother,' he says, 'what am I gaunna do stayin wi you mysel sittin here in the house and them awa enjoyin theirsel round the country. I'll go wi them, go with them tae.'

'Well,' she says, 'I'll pack up a wee bit something fir ye tae eat the morn and see what yese can dae.' She raiked up the barrel and she got a puckle meal and she said, 'I'll mak three wee bannocks for ye, three o' them. I'll make yese ane each. And I'll fry yese a wee bit bacon, a wee collop o' ham and yese can tak it wi yese.' So she made two big anes and she hadna much left. But the third ane she made was on'y a wee bannock.

So they rose in the morning and had their breakfast. They packed two-three bits o' things they needed on their backs and she said, 'I had tae roll ye up something to tak wi yese on the road, it's a lang road yese 's gaun, there may no be a house on the road, ye may get nothing alang it.' She says, 'Sandy, there's a bannock—what do ye want? Dae ye want that wee ane wi a bless or dae ye want me tae gie ye that big ane wi a curse?'

'Tsst,' he said, 'curse and a blessin, I'm no wantin nae blessin—I'll take the big ane wi the curse. Curse as much as ye want to, gie it to me, I'll take the big ane!' He got his big bannock and his bit collop o' ham, rolled it up. In his pocket wi it. Come Willie's turn.

'Willie,' she says, 'there's two bannocks there. Which ane do ye want? Dae ye want the big ane wi a curse or the wee ane with a bless?'

'Tsst, curses and blesses,' he said, 'gie me the big ane! I'll need it.' She gied him the same. Come Jack's turn.

'Well, Jack, son,' she says, 'ye're gaun awa tae leave yir auld mither, and God knows what'll happen to ye.'

'Ah, Mother,' he said, 'I'll no be long awa. I'm no worried about them. But they'll need someone to watch them, because they'll definitely get into trouble. Ye ken what like they are. The carry on they keep when they're out o' yir sight. I'll go wi them fir a while and see what happens.'

She says, 'Jack, that's all that's left, the're only one wee bannock. Ye'll hae to tak it.'

'Ah, Mother,' he said.

'Well I'll tell you,' she said, 'you got it wi a blessin.'

He said, 'Thank you very much, Mother, thank you very much. And I'll come back to see you. And ony shillings I get, I'll save 'em up and bring 'em back to ye.'

Right, away the three o' them goes. But they wandered on and they wandered on and they wandered on, and on and on and on. Oh, they must hae travelled for about fifteen or sixteen miles.

Sandy says, 'I'm gettin kind o' hungry.'

Jack says, 'I'm gettin hungry tae.' Willie says the same thing.

Sandy says, 'Come on, we'll sit down, we'll bide here and we'll kinnel a fire and hae something to eat.' So they sat doon and they ate their bannocks and wee collops o' bacon, whatever they had. They sat a long long while. 'Look,' Sandy says, 'if the three o' us keeps together, we'll never get a job. The're nae place is gaunna gie three young men a job. We'll hae to split up if we want to get on in the worl, cause youse two is on'y a haud-back tae me.'

Willie says, 'I'm no carin, I can look after mysel.'

Jack says, 'Aye, youse can take care o' yirsel! But can youse look after yirsel?'

'Oh aye,' he says, 'we can look after wirsels. We dinnae need the likes o' you tellin us how tae look after wirsels. Ye'll never get naething, you'd be better gaun back to yir auld mither. Ye should never hae left her in the first place!' So they start arguin. They argued away for about half an hour. But anyway, they got it settled.

And Sandy says, 'Well, we'll push on anyway before it gets dark.' They pushed on and pushed on and pushed on. But it was just comin to evening. The first thing they came to at the roadside was a great big antheap. And the ants are all busy workin. Willie takes a look.

'Boys,' he said, 'the're bad fun! We can have some good fun wi those ants! Any o' youse got a match? We can set fire tae it!'

'Oh no,' Jack said, 'for God's sake, dinnae touch these things! Boys, ye'll no believe it, but I'm tellin ye—that's a heap o' witches. A heap o' witches there, and they all gather together at a certain time o' the year tae talk over their spells and the bad things they've done. And if youse go near them bad luck'll follae youse!' So he got them coaxed and they left the ants alane.

They travelled on about another mile. They came to this old fence, an old dyke it was. There were about fifteen swallows sittin on the dyke. Chatterin, chittin, chatterin and whistlin away.

Willie said, 'Boys, the're a bad shot! Get two-three stanes, we'll see wha can knock the first swallow off the top o' the dyke!'

'Oh dinnae, dinnae, dinnae!' says Jack. 'Boys, youse dinnae ken.'

Willie says, 'Now dinnae start that crack again about witches and warlocks and things!'

Jack says, 'That's worse! That's wizards. They gather every year fae all over the country. Listen to them the way they're talkin! The're some forent ones among them.' Oh, the swallows is twitterin away. 'Listen to them,' he said. 'They're wizards and they're gathered together for a meeting. If youse touch them, I'll guarantee ye, they'll cast a spell on ye, maybe turn ye intae a stane or something!' See, Jack was awfae good that way, good natured he was. So he got them coaxed and they left the swallows alane. Oh, they went a bit farther. They wandered on. It was just beginning tae get dark. They came doon tae this burnside and they sat doon tae tak a rest.

Willie said, 'Boys, we cannae gae nae further the night.'

'Ah,' Jack said, 'we cannae bide here! We'll have tae go on.'

Willie says, 'Look, there's a salmon! Come on! Look at it, look at it, there's something wrang wi it. It cannae swim very much!' And this great big salmon's lyin on its side, and it's gaun back and forward at the side o' the burn. Willie looks at it, says, 'Boys, we can kill that. We could cook it and roast it for wir supper!'

Jack says, 'Boys, boys, boys, hae yese got nae sense ataa? Dae ye see that? That's a king, an enchanted king frae the sea. And he's up there for a rest. And if yese touch him, I'll guarantee ye, God knows what'll happen tae yese. The best thing yese can dae is tae lea it alane.' So Jack gaes doon and he taks it and he puts it away back into a deep pool. 'Away ye go,' he said to the salmon. And to the boys, 'Never touch a salmon! A salmon's a sacred fish. Kings all

25

turns into a salmon during the summer and they come up for a run up the burn.' So he got them coaxed and they let it go. Away they go.

But they travelled on for about another mile and they came to this wee wood at the roadside. And they sat down. 'Boys,' Willie said, 'this will never do. We'll hev tae split up!'

So Sandy went over, he said, 'I'll tell ye what tae do. Look around youse, boys, the're three roads here. Now the're a road gaun that way, that's a main road, that must go into a toon. We cannae be far frae a toon noo. And there's another road gaun straight on, that gaes oot to the country. And there's another auld road, an old cart track. Somebody's cart must gae by somebody's farm. There must be an auld farm up that way somewhere. We'll lie doon here and we'll sleep. Whatever direction that wir feet's facin in the morning when we rise, each ane'll hev tae tak that road!' So they made a bargain.

'Right,' says Jack.

So they cut some branches and they made a bed tae theirsel, and they all lay doon. Jack he fell sound asleep. Willie fell sound asleep. But Sandy during the night he wakened up when the boys were asleep. He took Jack's feet and he turned them round and he faced them tae the auld cart road, put them doon that road. He took Willie's feet, and he faced Willie's feet away by the country road. And he faced his ain feet by the toon road and he lay doon and fell sound asleep.

So he's lying like this in the morning and he said, 'Right, boys, waken up, waken up!' They all sit up, you see. 'Now,' he said, 'do ye see the way yir feet's facin?'

'Aye,' Willie said, 'my feet's facin away bi the country, away that way. I might get a job, I'll gae that way.'

And Sandy said, 'Aye, my feet's facin on the main road by the toon. I'll gae to the toon.'

And poor Jack he looked all around him, and there was thes two woods gaun up this way. Two big woods and this

26

old cart road gaun away up bi among the rocks ower this hill. His feet was facin there.

'Jack,' he says, 'the're nothing for it, that's yir road. Ye'll hev to go that way!'

'Ah well, boys,' he said, 'I cannae help it. But I'll tell ye what I'll dae wi ye. I'll gae up that road and youse go the way youse is gaun. We'll bid good-bye. But,' he said, 'we'll make a promise before we go. We'll meet at wir mother's in a year and a day and see how we get on. Back at wir mother's hoose in a year and a day.'

'All right,' they say.

And Jack said, 'See who's the wellest off. There might be a farm up that road, I might get a job. Pro'bly if I get a job I'll stay there for a while and push round about. But back at my mother's in a year and a day ye'll hev tae be.'

'All right!' So they shook hands, bade each other farewell and away they set. So we'll start with Sandy first.

Sandy wanders away in, oh, he's got about three miles tae travel away into this toon. In he goes, searchin here, searchin there for a job. Nah, couldna get a job nae place, couldna get a job. He meets this old man. He says to him, 'Old man, ye ken whaur a body could get a bit work around here?'

'Nah,' he says, 'ye'll no get nae work out here, laddie. Everybody's away.'

He says, 'Everybody's away where?'

'Ah, everybody's away,' he says. 'The're naebody here. Only the auld folk's here in this village. Aa the young men's awa. Ye'd think a young man like you'd be awa tae.'

He says, 'Awa where?'

'Away oot to the big main city,' he says, 'searchin for the young princess' beads and her ring.'

'Tsst,' Sandy said, 'beads and ring! What're you talkin about beads and ring? I dinnae ken naething.'

'Well,' he said, 'look, the king o' this country hes got a lovely daughter. And before her mother dee'd she gev her a string o' pearls and a gold ring. And she was oot walkin wi her father and she lost the pearls. The next day she was oot in the boat wi her father, and she lost the ring. And hit belanged to her mother. She's breakin her heart for it. And she swore that she would marry the first man, young man, that would get her the pearls and the ring. And the king would give him half his kingdom. So that's where all the young men are.'

'Tsst,' Sandy says, 'hoo do you get there?'

'You just hev tae keep gaun till ye get on the main road,' he says. 'And see hoo ye get on. Jist keep askin and they'll tell ye about it. But it's a long, long way away.'

'No me,' says Sandy, 'I'm no gaunna bother. I'll knock about the toon for a while and see if I get mysel a bit job. I'm no gaun tae look for nae ring, where was I gaunna get a ring? I'm no walkin aroon aa day lookin for nae ring or beads or pearls or whatever they are.' So he never bothered.

Old man says, 'Suit yirsel.'

But Willie he set sail to the crossroads. And he wanders in and wanders in this long country, up hill and doon brae and up hill and doon brae and he travels on and on and on and on. Till he comes to this hoose at the roadside. There's an auld man sittin by the dyke.

He says to the man, 'Hoo far is it to the toon, first toon?'

Old man says, 'Laddie, laddie, you've a long road to the toon.'

'How far will it be?'

'Oh well, it's twenty mile onyway. You'll no get there tonight. But whaur are ye gaun?'

He said, 'I left my mother about a week ago, and I'm on the road.'

'Why, you're a big, strong lookin man!' he said. 'Ye'll be able to get work. I'm a woodcutter,' the old man says, 'an' I'm just lookin for a laddie about your age or about your build tae give me a help with the wood. And ye can stay in the house wi me. Ye'll get yir meat in the hoose. I'll gie ye yir pay, a good pay if ye work wi me in the wood. I cannae get naebody tae work for me. I've tried for a young lad but they're all away.'

Willie says, 'Whaur are they awa tae?'

So he up and tells him. He says, 'They're away tae the king's castle, tae the palace tae search the moors and the lochs.'

Willie says, 'What fir?'

He said, 'For the princess' ring and her beads. They belanged to her mother. She's breakin her heart for them and she's took to bed and she'll no rise. And the king's gaun off his heid.'

'Tsst, ach well,' Willie says, 'whaur am I gaunna get beads and ring? I'm no interested. But anyway, I'll tak ye up on yir job. I'll work awa wi you.' So Willie goes and he works wi the old man.

But Jack when he bade good-bye to his two brothers he set sail up the old cart track. And he's listenin to the birds whistlin and he's watchin a squirrel hidin nuts in a hole. Happy-go-lucky, no botherin atall, naething botherin him. He wandert on and wandert on and wandert on. He came to a wee bird wi a broken wing on the side of the road. He lifted it, sorted its wing and put it sittin o' top o' the dyke. 'There ye are,' he says, 'nae beasts'll get ye sittin there.' But he must hae travelled on about two mile and he came to this wee path. He says, 'There must be a house doon here someway.' It was at the side of this wood, down the side of this wood. And he gaes doon, and the first thing he meets doon this path is an old woman. She was cuttin sticks, you see. And she had this great bundle o' sticks tied with a rope. He walks over to her.

He said, 'Mother, excuse me, I was wonderin how far is it to the farm?'

She says, 'Laddie, whaur did ye come fae?'

He said, 'I cam up frae the main road, I left my mother about a week ago, and I'm oot just lookin for work.' She was an old, old woman. He said, 'I thought there were a farm up this road.'

'Aye, laddie,' she says, 'the're three farms on this road. If ye keep on this road right oot, follae it past the first farm, past the second farm, ti you come to the third farm. Pass that and ye'll gae on to the main road again, and it'll tak ye intae the toon.'

But Jack says to the old woman, 'Look, Mother, what are ye doin?'

She said, 'I'm gettin sticks for my fire for the wintertime. Ye get an awfa snow here in the wintertime, ye need an awfa sticks in.'

'Well, Mother,' he said, 'with the size o' the bundle of sticks you've got, I doot you'll no manage that. I'll tell ye what I'll do, if you could mak me something to eat, I'll carry you up some sticks that'll dae ye for a long while.'

She says, 'Would ye do that? I've never seen many young men up this road. Hardly naebody ever comes up here.'

He said, 'I'll get you some sticks.' So he took the old woman's axe frae her and he start't choppin sticks. He said, 'Is it far to your house?'

'No, it's only just a hundred yard down the pad there.' She said, 'I'll go away doon and make you something to eat.'

'Right,' he said, 'Mother.' Jack makes a great big bundle o' sticks, carries it doon, puts it in the stick shed, and goes back for another ane. And back for another ane, three bundles.

The old woman comes out, shouts him in. Takes him in, oh, she gives him a good feed. He says, 'Mother, what do you dae here?'

She says, 'I keep hens, and I sell a puckle eggs. Will ye no bide with me and stay wi me and work? I could gie ye a job. You're a nice laddie, a good laddie. And I ken you're a clever laddie and a good laddie by the look o' ye, the way you helped me today.'

'Nah, Mother,' he said, 'I was thinkin about pushin on.'

30

'Aye,' she said, 'you'll be gaun wi the rest o' them I suppose. Ye'll be gaun wi the rest o' them.'

'Whaur tae, Mother? What "rest"?'

'Did you no hear the news?' she says.

'What news?'

'Well,' she says, 'the're the king o' the country, about twenty mile frae here is his castle. And he owns all this country right round. They only had ane daughter i' their life, and she was awfae devoted to her mother. And her mother before she dee'd gev her this double string o' pearls and a gold ring. It was the last thing that her mother ever gev her before she died. And she was oot with her father walkin one day when she lost the pearls, the string broke and she lost every single pearl. The next day she was oot wi her father in the boat fishin—because her father took her every place to keep the thocht o' her mother deein aff her heid. And she was leanin ower the side o' the boat and the ring fell ower the side of the boat. And she's breakin her heart, she's took to bed for it and she cannae get it. The king swore that he would give half o' the money in his kingdom tae anybody that could get the ring and the pearls back fir his dochter.'

'Oh,' Jack said, 'it's a hard task, Mother, tae get that.'

'Ah,' she said, 'it could be done, though, it could be done. If ye kent the right spot it could be done. *You go and try onyway, Jack, and I doubt you'll manage, and I wish you the best of luck.*' (This was an auld henwife, you see! And auld henwives were supposed to be witches in them days.) So she makes him up some stuff, some meat tae carry wi him and bids him good-bye.

Jack bids good-bye to the old woman and away he goes, travels on and on. He passes the first farm, passes the second farm and passes the third farm, and oot to the main road. He walks along to this place and he gaes in this wood, he lies doon and he sleeps for the night. But oh, he was lyin in this wood and it was cold and he couldna sleep, he tossed and turned

31

all night. But he gets up early in the morning and he eats a bit meat that the old wife gien him and he sets on the road. He travels on and travels on and travels on till he comes to the toon. He lands into the toon—oh, there were folk of all description! There were old men, young men, beggars, ladies, women all wanderin through thes moors.

So Jack stops and he says to this old man, 'What's all the folk lookin for?'

'Oh, do ye no ken, laddie, what folk's lookin fir?' He says, 'See thon big castle up on the hill yonder?'

He says, 'Aye.'

'Well,' he says, 'that's where the king stays and his young dochter. She's bedfast, breakin her heart for her mother's pearls. See thon fresh-water loch oot below the castle yonder? Well in the middle o' thon loch somewhere lies her ring, and it'll never be gotten. The're men out there divin and swimmin and tryin their best tae get it. It's worth a fortune, and mebbe the daughter forbyes! For anybody who could get it.'

'Oh,' Jack said, 'I cannae tell ye hoo they're gaunna get a ring oot o' that loch! But onyway, whaur did the princess lose the pearls?'

'Well,' he said, 'do ye see the rocks o' thon castle, sits up on thon rocks? Doon there on thon moor where you see aa thon folk wanderin about, well, it's somewhere in there.' But there must hae been two hundred-three hundred folk wanderin here wi sticks and hokin and pokin and lookin for thes beads.'

Jack says, 'Can onybody . . .?'

'Oh yes,' said the old man, 'onybody can go, laddie. I wish you the best o' luck. Onybody can wander. You may wander for a lifetime, but you might never get them! But it's up to yourself to have a go if you want.'

'Ach well,' Jack says, 'the're nae harm done. If the rest o' the folk's lookin, I might be lucky.'

He said, 'If ye could even get ane, well, if ye get ane ye'll ken whaur the rest is. They cannae be far awa. The string broke and they all went scatterin on the moor, and the lassie's breakin her heart for them.'

So Jack walks on and he wanders up. And he wanders doon, and he's wanderin here, he's kickin wee bits o' grass wi his feet and wee bits o' bark, and he's wanderin through bushes and heather and grass. Ach, he must hae wandered for two hours. Nothing. The folk began to pack up for the day. He's sittin wi his back against a tree, ti the last body passed by. The last body passed. And he's wonderin, he says, 'God, it would be lucky for me and my auld mother at hame if I found thes beads and the king gied me a few pound. I could go right back to my old mother right away and search for them two silly brothers o' mine and gie them two-three shillings and get them started on their feet. It would be a good help if I could get this.'

But onyway he's lookin doon, and creepin up the front o' his leg was an ant, a pishmill! Creepin up his leg! And he came wanderin up. And Jack was gaunnae knock it off like that, when it came right up to his knee and stopped. It sat on his knee. It sat up.

'Do ye remember me, Jack?' says the ant.

Jack leans ower and he says, 'What? What?'

He says, 'I'm an ant.'

'Oh,' he said, 'I can see you're an ant, but ants cannae speak.'

'But,' he said, 'I can speak! Ye dinnae remember me!'

'No,' he said, 'I dinnae remember you.'

'Think back,' he says, 'a while ago. You and yir two brothers—when you saved wir life frae gettin burnt to death wi yir silly brothers. They were gaunna put a match tae us. Only for you. You saved wir life. So me and my freends, we ken ye're here. And me and all my freends, the're thousands o' us, made up wir mind that we're gaunnae do ye a good turn. 'Cause you did us a good turn. You just sit there, Jack!' he said. 'And we ken what ye're lookin fir, ye're lookin fir the pearls. We ken where the pearls are. We've

33

passed them often through the grass. And you sit there, and we'll get the pearls tae ye!'

Tsst, Jack thocht he was dreamin. But anyway, doon goes the ant, creeps back doon on to his boot, on to the grass and disappears. Jack must hae sat for about ten minutes. And here they're comin in strings. Two ants tae a pearl between them! Every two ants were carryin a pearl. And they came right in atween his legs, and they dropped one after the other, one after the other, one after the other till they got every single pearl.

'There ye are, Jack,' he says. 'There's yir pearls and we wish you the best o' luck! One good turn deserves another!' And away go the ants!

'God,' Jack said, 'that's good! That's the pearls onyway.' Oh, was he glad noo! He says, 'At least he'll gie me something for this, a reward. Definitely, they're bound to gie me something.' Takes his wee hankie that his mother tied the bannock intae, his wee bannock wi the bless, ties the pearls intae it, ties it in a knot, puts them in his pocket. Oh, he's smilin tae hissel, all in his glory, he's got every single pearl.

Noo he walks doon. He said, 'I'll take a walk roon the side o' this loch and see what happens, tae see if it's deep. Hoo they can loss a ring in that loch I cannae . . . but it's bound to be in the bottom there somewhere.' So he walks along and he comes to this rock, and he's watchin this shingle roon the side o' this rock. He's sittin, 'Ach,' he said, 'I'll tak off my boots. Well, I'll wash my feet in the loch, as long as I'm sittin here.' Off with his boots and he's sittin on this rock. 'Before I gae up to the king's castle with the pearls, at least I get my feet washed!'

And he hears splash-splash, splash-splash, and he looks roon. Up comes this great big salmon, a big salmon about fifty pound. Right in, it cam right in beside his feet and it stopped. Put its nose up through the water.

He said, 'Remember me, Jack?'

'What?' says Jack.

He said, 'Ye remember me?'

'Nah,' he said, 'I dinnae remember you. You're a salmon!'

'Aye, I'm a salmon,' he said. 'But remember me? Ye saved my life when your two silly brothers was gaunna kill me and roast me! And you put me back into the pool and saved my life. One good turn deserves another! And I'll no forget ye.' He says, 'I ken what ye're here fir. Ye're here lookin for the princess' ring. In the bottom o' the sea oot there, in that loch oot there. I passed it about half an hour ago, and I'm gaunna get it to ye.' Jack was mystified. He didna ken what was wrong wi him.

He said, 'Would ye do that fir me? But you're a salmon, hoo can you speak?'

'Never you mind hoo I can speak,' he says. 'But I'm gettin you a present. You've done a lot for me and saved my life. One good turn deserves another.' Sweet—away he goes. Disappears. Jack, on wi his stockings, on wi his boots, sits a minute. Up comes the salmon. Ring in the salmon's mouth. Up he comes, nose oot o' the water, says, 'Jack, hold out your hand!' Jack holds it out and the salmon drops the ring in his hand. 'There ye are, Jack,' he says, 'and the best o' luck to ye! One good turn deserves another.'

Jack takes the ring. Oh, it was a beautiful ring, bonnie gold ring. Ties it in his hankie along wi the pearls, puts it in his pocket. He's away hustlin back, oh, he's as happy as a lark. 'Noo,' he said, 'they're bound tae gie me something! I wonder how them silly brothers o' mine's gettin on.' Up he goes, walks up to the castle. Right to the palace, there's two guards standin.

'Where are ye gaun,' he says, 'young man? I thought you'd be out wi the rest o' the people. Ye're allowed to hunt for the pearls and the ring, but ye're no allowed in here.'

He says, 'I want to see the king.'

Guard says, 'What dae ye want to see the king fir?'

Jack said, 'I want to see the king because I found the ring and the pearls.'

'You found the pearls and you found the ring—the likes o' you? How could you go in the middle o' that sea and find the ring?'

'Well,' he says, 'you take me to the king!'

The king's sittin in his big room on his throne inside the palace. One guard walks in. 'Yir Majesty,' he said, 'there's a man here says he has found the ring and the pearls.'

'What?' says the king. 'The ring and the pearls?' Noo he's thinkin aboot his wee lassie lyin bedridden, cannae rise for the thought o' this ring and thes pearls belanged to her mother. 'Fetch him in immediately! Bring him to me!'

He takes Jack in to the king. King looks, eyes him doon. 'Young man,' he says, 'dae you know what's gaunna happen to you if you're tellin me lies?'

Jack bended on his knees. 'No, Yir Majesty, I'm no tellin ye nae lies,' he said. 'I found yir pearls—the're sixty-three pearls.'

'Right,' says the king, 'the're sixty-three pearls.'

'And every one is the same size.'

'Right,' says the king, 'every one's the same size.'

'And,' he said, 'a gold ring with six diamonds intae it. And all the diamonds are the same size.'

'Right,' says the king. 'Have you got them?'

'I have them.' And Jack opens the hankie and he hands them to the king.

The king immediately calls for the lady-in-waiting to come in. He says, 'Carry down the princess.'

Two maids ran up, they carried down the princess, put her sittin in the chair. He walked over tae her, he said, 'Daughter, I've got a great surprise for ye. There's a young man here hes brought you a great present and I think your worries'll be over for the future.'

'No, Daddy, it couldn't be!' she said.

He says, 'He's got your pearls and your ring.'

36

And the princess was that overjoyed she stood up! And she ran over to Jack and she put her two arms roon his neck and kissed him. She kissed him. The king was lookin at this, see?

So the king said, 'Right, this man must get the reward.'

'No, Daddy,' she said, 'I want him to stay for a couple o' days. We must be good to him, because he did a great thing for me.'

And when the king saw his daughter was so hale and so well and so healthy after gettin her ring and her pearls back, he said to Jack, 'You can stay for a while and we'll look after ye.'

Jack stayed for a week, and the princess fell in love wi him. They were out walkin i' the garden, oh, she was happy as the day is long! She was just like a singin bird this princess noo since she got her ring back. But the king wasna pleased, he wasna pleased wi this. And one day he was oot watchin and he saw the two o' them kissin at the back o' the dyke.

He said, 'That man's never gaunna marry my daughter. He's no good enough to marry my daughter. I don't know what he cam off o'.' So one day he called for Jack to come in. The king sat and had a long talk to him. The king said, 'I see you get on very well wi the princess.'

'Yir Majesty,' said Jack, 'I get on very well wi the princess. In fact, I love the princess.'

'Oh, you love the princess?' he said. 'Well, the princess is my daughter.'

'Well, Yir Majesty, I know she's yir daughter,' he said. 'I'm only a poor man. I'm only a poor man and . . . but I love your daughter. I love the princess and the princess loves me!'

'Well,' said the king, 'I owe you a lot o' money. In fact I owe you a terrible lot o' money, and you'll get the money but you cannae get the princess.'

'Well, Yir Majesty, if I cannae get the princess,' Jack said, 'I'm no wantin yir money.'

37

'Well,' says the king, 'ye are a good man, right enough.
Ye are a good man. But I'll tell ye, I'm a game man, and
if ye're as game as me I'll make a deal wi ye. I'll give ye
a task. And if you can fulfill this task that I'm gaunna give
you . . .' and he called for the princess. He told the princess
in the room wi Jack, 'Jack says he loves ye!'

'Yes, Daddy,' she says, 'and I love him. And we would
like yir permission to get married.'

'Well, daughter,' he said, 'I've nothing against him, he's a
young man, he's a good-lookin young man. You love him and
you want to marry him. But first he's got to fulfill a task to
me to prove that he's a good enough man for ye.' The king
was fly, ye see, fly.

Jack says, 'Yir Majesty, what would I have to do?'

'Well,' he says, 'look, in a faraway kingdom very far from
here lives my brother. And I never saw him for five year, and I
never got word o' him for five year. So if you're gaunna marry
my daughter, I want you to take him a letter invitin him tae
come back here fir the wedding. You deliver that letter and
come back here after you deliver the letter, you can marry
my daughter wi my permission. But if you don't deliver the
letter, you'll never marry my daughter.' Noo the king knew
that where Jack had to go it was impossible to cross this
place. He had to cross a desert and he had to cross a river
and cross this place that was fortified with robbers. The're
no man that the king ever knew got through this place. And
Jack had to go through jungles and things to get through
this land. And the king said to hissel, 'He'll never make it.
Nobody could make it where his brother stayed.'

'Okay,' says Jack, 'I'll take your letter.'

So the king is false, you see. The king sits down, writes the
letter, seals it with wax, gives it to Jack. He says, 'Noo you'll
tak this to my brother. When you bring me back an answer—
it must be an answer frae my brother in writing—then you
can marry the princess with my blessing. But,' he says, 'I'm
tellin ye, it's five hundred mile through the roughest country

in the worl you must go. And if anything happens to ye, it's
yir own fault!'

'Right,' says Jack, 'I'll go.'

Away Jack set sail and he travelt and he travelt and he
travelt. He travelt and he travelt and he travelt, he must
hae travelt for about a hundert mile. On the road for days.
But oh, it's gettin rougher as he's gaun, rougher and rougher
and rougher. At last he cam to this sea, a ragin sea. And
he had to cross. No boat, no nothing atall. Now the king
knew this. But he had to cross this sea to the land on the
other side, where the king's brother stayed. So Jack's sittin
wonderin and sittin wonderin and wonderin what tae dae.

'Nah,' he said, 'I've got to give up, it's hopeless. I'll never
cross here.' When down comes this thing from the sky—fwit—
'tweet-tweet'. Pops on his knee—a swallow. Right on his knee,
lands. A wee swallow. Jack said, 'There must be something
chasin ye. Was there a hawk chasin ye, wee bird?' He looks
all round about him, in case there was.

This swallow says, 'Aye, ye mightna look roon, Jack, the're
nae hawk chasin me!'

Jack says, 'What was that?'

He said, 'Do ye remember me?'

Jack said, 'You're a swallow. A bonnie wee swallow.'

'Ah, but do ye remember me?' he said. 'Think back a
long long time ago. You and yir two brothers. When me and
my friends were sittin on the fence when they were wantin
to throw stanes at us, see who could knock the first o' us
doon. I cam to help you—one good turn deserves another. I
know what ye're here fir. You're to deliver that letter. But
you could never deliver that letter. Never in a million years.
But I'm gaunna deliver it fir ye! And I'm gaunna bring back
an answer.' He says, 'You sit here ti I come back! And don't
move.'

'Well, thank God,' says Jack, 'I've got some help, someone
to help me.'

The wee swallow takes the letter in its beak and set sail, and it's away. Oh, it flies and flies and flies and flies, you know. Within hours it was across the sea and ower this jungle and ower this desert and right up to the king's castle on top of this big rock! Lands right at the window. And just as it lands on the window, who is there at that fearin time but the king! And he looks and he sees this wee bird. It pops in and it drops the letter. And the king lifts it. It was addressed to him. The swallow still sits. And the king reads it, 'Dear Brother, I'm sending a man with a letter to you giving you an invitation to come to my daughter's wedding. Would you kindly come?'

The king says, 'That's my brother. I've never seen him for five year. His daughter's gettin married. I'll have to go and see him!' Quick as he could write he writes another wee note, signs it, seals it, hands it to the swallow. Wee swallow takes it in its neb and away it goes, sets sail. Jack's still sittin.

In comes the swallow, lands back upon his knee. 'There ye are, Jack,' he says. 'There's yir answer fir ye.'

'By God,' Jack says, 'you werena long!'

'No, I wasna long,' he says. 'But you helpit me and I'm helpin you. Noo you take that back to the king!' Away Jack goes.

Wanders and travels and travels and travels all that road back. And he has this letter in his pocket. And he wouldna part with it. He couldna sleep at night in case somebody would come and take it frae him! And he travels on and he travels on and he travels on, travels back and travels back, till he lands right back to the king's palace again. Up he goes tae the palace, and right to the same guard.

He says to the guard, 'I want to see the king.'

Guard said, 'What do you want to see the king for? A raggy thing like you?' Jack's clothes were all torn, ye ken, wanderin the road for days. And his boots were all torn and he had a beard on him, never had a wash for weeks.

He said, 'I want to see the king, I've got a letter for him!'

'Oh, you've got a letter for him?' he says. In goes the

40

guard. He says, 'Yir Majesty, there's a young man at the gate. He says he has a letter for ye.'

'Aye,' says the king, king thinks back. 'That'll be him back with the same letter. He could never make it, I kent he would never dae it,' he says. 'I kent he couldna dae it. There's nae man could dae it, cross the Red Sea with my letter. Send him in!' says the king.

In goes Jack. 'Yir Majesty,' he said, 'there's yir letter!'

'Aye, I kent you couldna mak it,' he says. 'My son, I knew you couldn't make it. That's the same letter . . .'

'No, it's no the same letter you gied me. You never gied me this letter,' Jack says. 'You better read it.'

King opens it and reads it. He says, 'You did go to my brother's! But how did ye dae it?'

Jack said, 'I did it.'

'Well, I'll tell ye one thing, if you did go, and went to my brother,' he said, 'and got that letter from him, you are a good man! And I think ye're fit enough to marry my daughter!' He calls two men. 'Take him away and get him bathed and get him scrubbed and get him plenty new clothes—the're gaun to be a wedding in this place!'

So they took Jack away, gev him a good bath and gev him a new set o' clothes. And the princess was delighted to see him back, got her father's permission. All the plans were laid for the wedding and everybody in the country was invited to come to the wedding. Everybody's invited! So Jack got married to the princess, and the king gev him all his money.

And the king says, 'Look, do ye want to stay here with me? Or do ye want to go and buy a castle to yourself somewhere else?'

Jack said, 'Yir Majesty, the first thing I'd like to dae, before anything, is me and my wife go for a honeymoon.'

King said, 'Where dae ye want to go?'

He said, 'I would like to go and see my old mother.'

He said, 'Where does your mother stay?'

41

'Oh, a long road frae here,' he says. 'Very, very far awa fae here.'

'Well,' the king says, 'I'll give ye the best coach, and take the best horses, and take as many footmen and as many couriers as ye want with ye.'

'Oh,' said Jack, 'I'll just take a coach and a pair o' horses, and me and the princess my wife'll go and see my mother.'

So they took a royal coach and two white horses. Four or five men went wi them to help them on their way, in case robbers would attack them. And away they go. They set sail the next day and they're on the road for about a week. And they land back to their old mother's hoose.

By this time now Sandy had wandered round the town, got hissel into trouble and in jail. He'd been in the jail for six months and he got fed up knockin roon the toon, and he cam hame. The minute he landed hame he cam in, his auld mother said tae him, 'Whaur were you aa the time?'

'Ah, Mither,' he says, 'I was better here gettin sticks tae ye! At least I got my meat fae you. When I went into the toon and fell in wi bad folks, and ah, I got into trouble, got the jail. And I got sick fed up, I cam hame. I'm no gaun awa nae mair! I'm stayin.'

She says, 'What happened tae yir other two brothers?'

'Oh God knows,' he said, 'what happened to my two brothers. I dinnae ken.'

But the next day who turned up but Willie! Old mother's glad to see him, took him in, gied him his tea. 'What happened to you, Willie?'

'Oh me,' he says, 'Mother, I'm aa right. When I left, when Sandy and Jack left me, I fell in wi an auld woodcutter. An I workit away wi him for about ten month. And the auld man dee'd, and I married his daughter. I got the business to myself. And I'm just here tae see ye the day. We promised Jack we'd be back in a year and a day, and the morn the year and the day's up. I thocht I would come back and see how yese 's gettin on.'

42

'By God,' says Sandy, 'you've done all right for yourself! That's mair than I can say for me. I got naething. I done nothing, I couldna even get a job.'

But the old mother said, 'That's no hit! What happened to poor wee Jack? What happened tae him? Whaur did he go tae? What did yese do on him?'

So they up and they tellt their mother the crack—hoo they turned their feet. Sandy said, 'It was me, I turnt the boys' feet. If we hadna done it we'd hae been luckier.'

'Well,' she says, 'if Jack's livin, he'll be here the morn. If he said to you he'll be here in a year and a day—he'll be here!'

But anyway, they went to their bed. In the morning, a lovely summer's morning, the old wife was up. She made some breakfast to the boys. Just about ten o'clock she looks up and here's this coach comin. Oot comes the two boys.

'Mither,' Sandy said, 'here's a coach comin. And they're royalty bi the looks o' them. That's a royal coach, I ken the way it's comin, the horses, the way the harness is shinin.'

Willie says, 'Mother, it's no often you see a coach comin this way to your place. Wha could it be?'

She said, 'I hope it's not that wee brother o' yours, got hissel in trouble. He promised to be back the day, and I bet you a pound that's him comin to tell us about it. Mebbe he's got hissel in serious trouble—mebbe he's done some kind o' wild harm.'

But up comes the coach, six riders wi it, stops in front o' the wee croft door. Mother's standin, Willie and Sandy are standin at the door. Out steps Jack, oh, dressed like a young gentleman, his young princess wi him.

'Well, boys,' he said, 'it's me, I'm back. It's your brother Jack, I'm back! And this is my wife, princess.' Oh, the lady bowed. They shook hands all around. And he said, 'I cam back to keep my promise, a year and a day. A year's up the day, I cam to see my old mother. But I havena long to wait, I can only stay for minutes, half an hour at the most.

43

But onyway, I kept my promise. And how did youse get on? I'm all right, I'm married to the princess and I'll be gaun away back in a short time, back tae her father's kingdom a long road frae here. But before I go I want one thing tae dae. I must take my old mother back wi me. You've got to come back wi hus, Mother, and we'll look after you the rest o yir days.'

'Well,' says Willie, 'I'll no be stayin here either. I'm gaun away back the day masel tae. I'm well off, I'm married, I've got a nice business o' my own, a woodcuttin business and I've got a nice young wife. I'm due home onytime.'

And Sandy says, 'What's gaunna happen to me? What's gaunna happen to me?'

'Look, Jack,' Willie said, 'did he tell ye what he done thon night when we were at the crossroads?'

'No, he never tellt me what he did.'

'Well,' he said, 'he turnt wir feet, and he faced yir feet to the hill. He faced my feet to the country and his ain feet to the toon. And look at him noo! And look at us. We're well off. Ye're well off, ye're married to the princess. I've got a good wood contractin business. And he's nothing. Ye ken what he deserves?'

'Aye,' says Jack, 'I ken what he deserves! He deserves my mother's old hoose for the rest o' his days. Let him bide into it till it rots!' So Sandy was left with his mother's old hoose. And Willie went back to his wife and his business. Jack took his princess and his old mother hame wi him to the kingdom and they lived happy ever after. And that's the last o' the story!

JACK AND THE WEE BALL OF THREAD

This story was told to me a long long time ago when I was only about ten years old. The storyteller was an old cousin of my father's, an old man by the name of Willie Williamson. Willie could neither read nor write and he travelled with his wife, his two daughters and his son. He played his bagpipes in the summertime wandering Argyll and Perthshire and Dumbarton . . . many parts of Scotland. And his fame had spread far and wide as a storyteller. Where he got the stories I could not tell you. He was in the 1914 War, and he got his ankle shot off. Maybe he brought some of these stories back from Germany, maybe from the 1914 War. But he was one of the finest storytellers I'd ever met in all my life. When I was a child he came for visits to Furnace in Argyll and put his little tent up by the riverside, across the river from where we stayed in the woods. I can remember old Willie, his wife old Belloch and his two lassies and me and my little brothers and sisters sitting around the fireside, and gathering hazel sticks, putting them on the fire. He would say, 'Weans, dinna mak it too bright. Because if you mak the fire too bright, it'll no be the same. Save some because this is a lang story . . .' So tonight I'm going to tell you a wonderful story. It could have tooken place in Ireland, it could have tooken place in England, maybe in Scotland . . . it's hard to tell.

You see, a long time ago, long before your time and mine there wonst lived a king. Near his palace there was a small village

45

and everyone in the village worked for the king. Everyone loved and respected him because he was a good king. When he was middle-aged he married a young woman, who had been a princess or maybe a squire's or an earl's daughter. Nobody actually knows for the truth. But they were very happy together. And everyone in the village really loved the young bride. And of course so did the king! But the king's greatest ambition was to have a son, because as my story will tell you now he was in his late forties. And then after many weeks and months had passed, the couriers around the village gave out the news—the queen was expecting a baby. Oh, everyone was overjoyed, overjoyed to hear the queen was expecting! So as the weeks and months passed by, finally the great day arrived and the queen gave birth to a baby son.

The king called it an open holiday. He invited everyone from the village, from the far-out countries far and wide to come before him, he would give them the greatest enjoyment, the greatest party they ever had in their life! The palace grounds in these bygone days were surrounded by a wall, a great wall that separated it from the village. So the gates were thrown open and everyone was invited. There were feasting and singing and dancing and drinking. But as you know, along with fun the're always tragedies. Because the king had sent special invitations to the ones he knew best, the rich and the people of high degree.

But in the village there lived two old sisters. And they were never invited to the great party of the king's birth of his baby. Nobody gave much thought to the two old sisters, because these sisters were kind of outclassed by the villagers. People had said funny things about them, they were this, and they were that, they were witches and everything else. And probably, maybe a few words had got to the king that they were not very nice people to invite to the birth of his baby son. But after many days of feasting and dancing and drinking, everyone returned to their homes. The two old sisters had never turned up at the reception for the baby son's birth. The king never gave much thought to this at first. But after many weeks and months had passed, queer things begint to happen in the village. Fields of grain would catch on fire and burn for no reason. Trees would fall without wind across the roadsides. Cattle would stagger and die in the village. And nobody could know why.

Now, there were many stories told. People were saying maybe it's the cause of the old women, the two old sisters who lived together in a little cottage well out of the village. Everyone classed them as witches. They were not very nice people. When they came to the village they would talk to no-one, they would do their little bits of shopping and go home as fast as they could. No-one was allowed near their house, they never made nobody welcome near their house. And they both got a bad name in the village. But anyhow things begint to happen in the village that nobody could account for. And the king heard about these things. Trees are falling, fields of beautiful harvests are catching on fire! Healthy young animals are dropping dead and dying. Sheep are dying, cattle and horses are dying for no reason. People are getting sick—healthy people who had never had a day's illness in their life are getting sick. Who was causing all this trouble?

So the king had begun to hear all these stories come before him naturally from all the people. And by listening to this he was a little bit worried and upset. Not at the first! He just treated them as stories. But after things begint to happen in the village that no-one could account for, the king really felt it was about time he should do something about this. So naturally as you know every king in these bygone days, let it be a high king or a lear king or just a thane, which is just an earl or a duke, he had a wiseman in his palace who would be called when he had a problem.

He called his wiseman before him, 'Wiseman, what's going on in my country? Are there any reasons for all thes

47

problems? I hear stories coming from the village, from the
farmers, from the people who pays their taxes to me and
shares their grain and shares their animals with me . . .
What's the problem?'

'Well you see, my lord,' said the wiseman, 'the're many
stories.'

'What kind o' stories?' said the king.

'Well,' he said, 'it all lays doon to the blame of the two
old women you had never invited to your child's birthday.'

'What women?' he said.

'The two old sisters,' he said. 'My lord,' he said, 'people
say they are witches!'

The king said, 'Look, wiseman, the're no such a thing! I
don't believe in witches.'

'My lord,' he said, 'they are! Ye know, these women has
got magical powers, and,' he says, 'no-one can account for
anything else that's happening. It must be them!'

'Well,' the king said, 'I would like to bring them before
me and have a talk to them and see if the stories are true.'
Now the king was an honest man, a great king. Otherwise
his subjects would not have loved him. He was very honest
and very true. He said, 'Wiseman, I'll heed your warning.
I will send five o' my soldiers, and ae captain of my guard
to the old ladies and I'll bring them before me. And then I'll
ask them. They cannot lie to me! Should they lie to me it
will be worse on them.'

Now a year had passed since the birth of his baby son.
His baby son was a year old. And the queen loved her baby
son, she wouldna let him out of her sight. And so did the
king because he would be the future king of the country.
Anyhow, he sent the five soldiers and the captain of the
guards to bring in the old ladies that he could talk to them.
Just civilly talk to them and see what was the problem. He
wanted to meet them because they had never met. But when
he sent the captain of the guards and five of the soldiers to
the old ladies' little house well out of the village . . . they

lived in a kind of a wood far from the village . . . they were gone! The house was empty! There was not a soul to be seen around the house. It was completely empty.

So the guards came back. 'Master, my king, my lord,' the captain of the guards told the king, 'They are gone. The old women have flown. They're not to be found.'

'Well, send someone around the village!' he said. So the king sent the guards and the soldiers around the village. And they were asking questions where the old women had been, had went. But the old women were gone! They could not be found. 'Well,' the king thought to hisself, 'they must be guilty or they wouldn't have absconded or been gone away. Where could they have been?'

Now, to bring you to this palace: there was the palace sitting on the hillside, there was the small village under the palace and there was a river that ran past the village. But down in the hollow where the farmers and all the little people made their living from, there was a place known as the catacombs. Now this could have been some kind of a old volcano eruption. And it was full of caves and holes. Many sheep and cattle and people had vanished in these catacombs in times gone past. Now this was a place called *tabu*, no one would visit, no one ever was allowed near it. Because once you entered this cave there were potholes in it, a kind of a cavern.

So, as my story tells you they sent the soldiers far and wide to seek the old sisters. But the two old sisters could not be found in any way, they were gone. The king said, 'This is, this is strange. Where have they gone?' No one ever gave a thought to the catacombs, this volcanic eruption place where people never entered because the're pitholes and wells and great dungeons!

Anyhow, life went on as usual. Two weeks passed—no cattle died in the village, no one took sick, no one took ill, no trees fell. The king said, 'A little peace at last in the village.' For the two old sisters had gone. They had vanished. But then, one morning as my story tells you there was a terrible uproar in the palace.

The queen came screaming down from her bedroom—her baby son was gone! He was gone, he had vanished from the palace. Screaming to maids and footmen and cooks and butlers in the palace, searching high and low . . . her baby son was gone! Could not be found. Oh, the king tried to console the queen, 'Oh, he cannot be far away,' because he was only a year old. 'We will soon find him. Maybe there's been a mistake made, maybe some maid has took him or something and put him in another room.' But they searched the palace far and wide . . . the baby son was gone.

The king sent couriers through the village asking everyone had they seen any strangers round the palace? No one had seen anyone. He sent couriers far and wide. The queen was tearing her hair. The king was so upset, his baby son one year old was gone! The king offered, 'I'll give anyone anything they ask for if they can find my baby!' But no one could find his baby. Five days had passed, the queen tearing her hair and crying her heart out, the king so sad at heart. And then soldiers he'd sent far and wide returned empty handed. There was no sign of the baby. They searched the river, they searched everything! The baby son could not be found.

And then, says the king, 'There's only one thing for me to do . . . although I hate doing this because he's done so much for me in the past . . . I must call on Jack.' Now as you know in many stories Jack had helped the king, he had brought Ivan from The Black Thief of Slane. He had done so much for the king, and the king had felt that it was just too much to ask Jack to come wonst again. But he says, 'For the sake of my baby son, it must be.' So he sent a rider and a horse to where Jack lived.

Now Jack lived with his mother in a little cottage in the forest. And he cut a few firewood for his mother. He was very well off because he had worked for the king many,

many times; he had saved the king in a snowstorm, he had brought the king back, he had done many things in many stories for the king. And Jack and the king were great friends. Jack was busy cutting, chopping up firewood at his house for his mother's fire when he saw the rider. And he knew by the saddlebags and the sweat of the horse that the rider had come from the king. Oh, Jack and his mother had attended the birth of the king's baby son. Jack had saw the baby when he was just two-three days old, because everyone was invited to look on the baby. And when the rider came in to Jack he said, 'The king has sent for you, Jack.'

'Well,' Jack said, 'this must be something else, he must be in trouble.'

And the guard said, 'Well, I don't want to talk about it, but I'll let the king tell you hissel.' So he had a spare horse with him for Jack, because Jack never had a horse. And Jack said good-bye to his mother, climbed aboard the horse and rode back to the palace. And when he rode into the palace he was made welcome, because he was well known. And he was led right into the king's chamber. The king and queen sat with their tear-stained faces and her hair hanging down— she had never combed her hair or washed her face because she was too upset about her baby son.

And Jack bowed before the king, he said, 'My sire, my lord, you've called on me.'

He says, 'Jack, yes, I'm—I'm at, I'm at airts end.' The king was—tears were rolling down his cheek.

Jack said, 'What's the problem, my lord, my king?'

He said, 'Jack, you know my baby is gone!'

'Your baby is gone?' said Jack.

And then the king said, 'My baby is gone and it's breaking my queen's heart and my heart too. My baby's been gone now for six long days!'

Oh, Jack was very upset by this. He said, 'What happened, my lord?'

'Well,' he said, 'we've searched the valley, we've searched

51

the river, we've searched far and wide. And,' he said, 'no one can find my baby son. But—'

Jack said, 'Someone must be blamed, take the blame of this!'

'Well,' he said, 'yes, Jack, as far as the wiseman believes, and as far as the village believes,' he says, 'the two old sisters have got my baby!'

But Jack said, 'Can't you find them?'

He said, 'Jack, well, we've searched far and wide and,' he said, 'they seem to have gone to the catacombs.' And he said to Jack, 'You know I've sent soldiers there, some has returned and some has not returned.' He said, 'Now Jack, that's a terrible place. And if the old sisters are living in there,' he says, 'there's no way in the world that anyone's going to get near them.' He said, 'Jack, I only asked you here . . . have you a solution for my problem?' an' the king was in tears!

Well Jack thought, 'There must be a way into the catacombs . . . if they made their way, then there must be a way to find them.'

'But Jack,' he said, 'it's terrible. Could you do something for me?'

And Jack said, 'My lord, my king, of course! I'll try my best.'

'Jack,' he said, 'I'll give you anything. You know, I— I'm sorry to bring you here, but it's the sake of my baby son.'

Jack said, 'My lord, my king I will go.' So Jack bade the king farewell and told the king he would do his best. But Jack never went home to his mother. Jack went to an old friend who he knew very well, the old henwife. She'd been a great friend of Jack's. When Jack had a problem, Jack always went to the old henwife. Now she lived about two miles from Jack's mother's house in a little cottage, a little thatched house in the forest.

So he walked all the way from the palace with thoughts

52

in his heart, thoughts in his head, could she really help him or couldn't she? Where had the king's baby son gone? But he went to the old woman's house, he knew her well. Old Jenny was her name. And when Jack came to the house and knocked on the door she was busy having a wee cup of tea by the fireside. It was the old traditional fireside . . . when she heard a knock on the door she put on her mutch because she thought—she didn't get many visitors coming to see her. This might be somebody important! But when she came to the door it was Jack.

'Oh Jack, my son,' she said, 'it's you! What's the problem? Is your mother no weel or something? What's gaun on?'

'No, Jenny,' he said, 'that's no the problem. Did ye hear the news?'

'Aye,' she says, 'Jack, I heard the news. Isn't it sad?'

He says, 'I cam to seek yir help.'

She says, 'Jack, I know what you're seeking. But,' she said, 'look it's a big thing you're askin of me.'

'Well, Auntie Jenny,' he said (he called her Auntie), 'well you know I've worked for the king many times and I want you to help me wonst again.'

'Well Jack, come sit doon,' she says, 'I've got a wee drop tea in the pot here. And let's talk about it while we have a cup o' tea.'

So he told her the story about the soldiers searching far and wide through the kingdom for the baby son of the king. But no one could find him. They searched in the river and searched in everything and no one has seen him taken from the palace. And the maids were questioned, and the footmen were questioned and everyone, the guards, the soldiers— but no one could find an answer to the problem! He said, 'Auntie Jenny, do you believe that these old sisters were responsible?'

'Well,' she says, 'Jack, they could be. I remember them in my childhood, they're about the same age as me. And they're evil, evil women! I didna have much to do with them, but they're very evil. But I'll tell ye something, they're very powerful. You know,' she said, 'the king really upset them when he never invited them with you and me and your mother to the birth of the baby. And they're only trying to get their ain back on him now!'

He says, 'Auntie Jenny, do you think that they maybe took the baby there . . .'

'Well,' she says, 'Jack, the're only one place they could go to—that's the catacombs! And,' she says, 'ye ken, Jack, naebody'll ever make their way in there. The're caverns, the're pitfalls down in there an' the're wells under the ground. That's a volcanic eruption and it's full of water and it's full of everything. But a path leads through it,' she says, 'that I've heard aboot. And if they're in there, there's nae way anyone's going to get near them!'

'But,' he says, 'the king's—the baby son, the king's son will die!'

'Oh,' she says, 'they'll no let it die, Jack. *They'll no let it die,*' she said. Because she had powers!

He said, 'Auntie Jenny, you must help me! Because I'm going to the catacombs!'

'Well,' she says, 'Jack, if you're going to the catacombs, laddie, I've helped you many times, and I suppose the're nae way tryin to keep ye back if you've made up yir mind to go. So,' she says, 'I'll give ye all the help I can. Just a minute . . .'

So hangin on the wall by the fireside was a wee bag. Jack had seen the bag before because she kept all her needles and thread in her bag. And she went to the bag and she put her hand in, and she brought out a big ball of woollen thread. Oh, about half the size of a present day football. 'Now,' she says, 'Jack, look what I have here. Now I'm warning ye, this is the only way ye're ever gaunna get into the catacombs. What I want ye tae dae, laddie, for my sake and for yir mother's sake, and for the sake of the king and everybody else,' she says, 'the minute you enter that catacombs in the clift, there'll

54

be darkness. And ye'll never see where ye're gaun. *I want ye to take this ball o' thread with ye and the moment ye enter the catacombs I want ye tae wrap a wee bit roond yir hand and throw the ball before ye. And this ball'll lead you . . . but as you walk forward I want you to roll it up again. And it'll tak ye to wherever the two old women are. And, if ye should get the baby prince, look, if you should come to where the baby prince is with the two old sisters, the're one thing you must never do: you must never look back! Even gaun in or comin oot, ye must never look back!'* She said, 'Ye'll need it on the road in but ye'll no need to roll it up on the road oot; leave it behind ye when ye follow it oot. If ye get the baby and ye see the old sisters,' she says, 'I dinnae ken what ye're gaunnae dae when ye get there, but,' she says, 'remember, follae this ball o' thread whatever ye dae. Mak up yir mind, gaun or comin, dinnae look back!'

So Jack accepted the big ball o' woollen thread frae the old woman. And after a cup of tea, 'Noo,' she says, 'when ye get there, just put a little bit roond yir hand and throw the ball in front o' ye.'

He said, 'Aunt Jenny, what happens?'

'Dinnae you mind what happens . . . *I'll be with ye in spirit but no with ye in body.*'

So after his wee drink o' tea, he bade his old auntie . . . well, she was called his auntie, she was nae relation to him. And off Jack set tae the catacombs. Now remember about this, the catacombs: the palace sat up on the hill, a river ran in front of the palace, a big good-goin river ran down through the village, down through the valley, and the catacombs were down in the hollow below the valley. Jack had passed them many times. They were kind of a burned out volcano workins. But only one entrance! People had vanished there many times. The place was evil to the villagers, *tabu*, and this, thought the king, 's where the two old sisters had took refuge with his baby son.

So Jack made his way with the wee ball of thread in his

55

hand and he said, 'What's gaunna happen to this?' But he travelled on, he hadna far to go from old Jenny's house, down the valley past the village, down to the hollow—and there were the catacombs, the burnt out red clift face! All, one big entrance, but when ye entered this it was an evil, evil place!

So it was late evening by the time Jack got down. So he came to the entrance, an' he took the ball o' thread that the old henwife had gien him, he tied it roond his hand and he threw the wee ball on the ground as the old woman had told him. And to his amazement the ball began to move! It began to move . . . and travel on. And Jack stood in amazement. The ball was alive, it was travelling on. It was dark in these caverns, but Jack could feel his way with his feet. And now and again he would touch a stone and it would go over the side of this narrow path, he'd listen and hear it . . . plonk in water way below him. But as the ball moved on in the darkness, he rolled the thread round his hand, and on and on travelled the ball. On and on travelled the ball, and soon Jack had a big ball he had to take off his hand, and then roll it wonst again to make a ball. But he travelled on . . . and after many times through narrow passages and stones slipping with his feet falling, and hearing falling in water many feet below . . . this ball seemt to have a life of its own. It travelled on and Jack followed and he rolled it round his hand as it travelled on through thes passages into the catacombs. Jack thought in his life, 'Where in the world is it goin in the darkness?' But as he could feel the wee thread he followed it . . . travelled on. And then, when he had a ball as big as the ball he had left on the ground, he saw flickering on the wall, flickering on the wall. And his heart lightened up.

So Jack put the ball in his hand very carefully, and he walked into a cavern, a large cavern. There was a little burned out fire made of sticks by the wall. There were bones lying on the floor, old bones, skulls and skeletons lying on the floor. Heads with skulls lookin at him! The light

56

from a burning old torch made of oil on the wall. He was
in a large cavern! And he looked—there on a bed of rashes
lay two old women with long dark dresses. And they were
sound asleep. He looked, and there by their side wrapped in
an old coat was a wee baby, and a big old bowl full of milk
by its side. But the baby was sound asleep. Jack knew this
was the place where the two old evil sisters had escaped to
from the terror of the king, and had taken the king's son in
revenge. He looked over carefully, the two old sisters were
asleep, they were snoring. They were lying there, ugly old
crones, but they were sound asleep. And on a bed o' rashes
wrapped in a coat sound asleep beside an old stone bowl full
of milk lay the young wee baby son of the king.

Jack, with the thread rolled up very carefully in his hand,
and makin no noise so's he wouldna disturb the old women, he
picked up the baby very carefully. It never opened its eyes, it
was sound asleep. Maybe the old women had put a spell on it
or something, maybe they had put it to sleep through some of
their powers. But he picked it up, and he caught it in his arm
. . . 'Now,' thought Jack, as the old woman, the old henwife
had told him, he turned his back to the old women and he
threw the ball o' thread on the ground. Now he could not
roll up the ball o' thread with holding the baby in one hand.
But the old woman had warned him, he would have no need
to roll up the ball of thread anymore. He would just . . . so
he caught a handful of the thread an' he threw it down, put
his foot on it and he picked up a wee stone and he placed
it on a part of the thread. And then following it like a line
with the baby on his arm, he put his hand on the thread
and let the thread feed through his hand. And the ball took
off wonst again. And Jack followed it very quietly and soon
he was in darkness wonst again. The old women were still
asleep. Jack wanted to look back to see would they waken
up, but the old henwife had warned him, *Jack, for the peril
of your life don't look back.* He wanted to look back, but he
remembered the words of the old henwife, don't look back!

57

So with the wee baby clasped in his arms, he followed the ball of thread, fed it through his hand. The ball of thread travelled on and out through the caverns, circling, touching stones that fell and dropped. And he heard them splashing away miles down below him. He travelled the same journey as he had come in. And then, after some time he saw daylight. And Jack was relieved to see the daylight. When he reached the entrance the wee ball of thread ran out. And there it lay, Jack left it.

He hurried on his way up the hillside from the catacombs up to the village. And when the people saw him in the village they gathered in their dozens! When Jack reached the palace all the people of the village were behind him! And they rushed up to the palace. And into the palace he went, met with guards, he pushed them aside with his hands and he rushed in. There sat the king and the queen, and he placed the baby on the queen's arms—threw the old coat on the floor and placed the baby on the queen's arms! And to his amazement the wee baby opened its eyes, it smiled!

And the queen cuddled the baby to her arms and cried, 'Oh my darling, you are back!' weeping for joy.

The king didna know what to do. He threw his arms around Jack and he kissed Jack and he cuddled Jack and he said, 'You've done it, you've done something that no one could do! Where did you find him, where did you find him?'

Jack says, 'In the catacombs. There is a cavern in the catacombs.'

But the king said, 'He's still no safe, they'll come back again, Jack! They'll come and take him away again.'

Jack said, 'My lord, my sire,' he said, 'you know the're been evil doings in the village.'

He says, 'Jack, there's no solution. They'll come, take him away again! They spirited him away already. Why won't they do it again? They could, Jack,' he said, 'I don't know what to do.'

'Well,' Jack says, 'I know what to do.' He said, 'My lord,

58

get all your soldiers! Get all the digging instruments they have for digging the fields, digging the gardens, digging spades. Call in the village! Call in your subjects!'

And the king sent messages to everyone in the village and he called all his subjects, called all his soldiers. And they took their diggin tools that they had for diggin their gardens, diggin their fields. And the soldiers with their swords and their bayonets and everything they owned. 'Now, Jack,' he says, 'what's this?'

Jack said, 'Look, my lord, my king, there is a river runs by the palace and the river is higher than the catacombs. And,' he said, 'what we want to do, we want to dig a trench—from the river to the catacombs. But we'll start at the catacombs and we'll flood the whole place, drown them out for evermore. And you'll never have another problem.'

So, this was arranged. In the hundreds they gathered; people from the village who loved the king and who loved the king's son and knew all about these two old evil sisters who had done many things on them. So they all started at the catacombs and with their picks and their spades, whatever they had in these days and their swords and their daggers, they drove a trench from the catacombs up the valley, up the hillside to the river bank. There were people from all over the village—noblemen, lairds and dukes, soldiers, farmers, everyone helped. And after some time there was a deep trench leading up from the catacombs. When they dug the last little piece on the river bank, and then they broke away, the water started to rush down the little track they had made. Everyone cheered and raised their hands! The water was running down the valley, into that trench they had dug rushed part of the river. It ran as everyone stood. And the king sent soldiers to guard the catacombs that no one would escape, and they stood there for two days. Till at last the water began to glug back from the catacombs. No one could escape. And Jack had never left the king's side.

Now the king said to Jack, 'The catacombs are full. They'll never escape.'

'Well,' says Jack, 'they are gone for ever.' The water flooded the catacombs for evermore and the old sisters were gone.

So they closed the riverside, the part where they had sent the water down the valley so that no more water could get in. Because the catacombs had been flooded for three days, it was full. They let the river flow, natural down the valley as it always done, on its journey.

The king was overjoyed and so happy to have his baby son back. He knew the old evil sisters were gone for evermore. But tonight they were going to have a great party. And they invited Jack, they invited Jack's mother and they invited the old henwife. For three long days they had a great get-together. They sang and they danced as usual. And the baby son of the king had never suffered one single thing. He was as right as a drop o' rain. And the queen was so happy to have her baby son back. And the king was so pleased that now the old evil sisters were gone for ever.

So after the feasting and dancing the king said, 'Well, Jack, I must thank you wonst again for doing this wonderful thing for me. I hope I never have any cause to call on you again. *But you never know, something may happen in the future!* And,' he says, 'Jack, for your work I'm going to give you one of my finest white horses that I have in my stable. And,' he said, 'for your old friend, the henwife, I'm going to give her a hundred balls of the finest wool!' And that is the end of my story.

JACK AND THE FACTOR

There are many different versions of this tale. I have four versions. In some the villain is the laird who owned the house that Jack lived in. But I like this one about the factor best. It's older than others I have heard. Another popular story by the same title is about Jack and an old goat called 'Factor', and how Jack mistakenly kills a real factor. But in my story Jack is the trickster, he is Jack the clever one!

Jack and his mother lived in an old cottage by the side of the forest that was owned by the local laird. But the laird had a factor who was very strict. Oh, the factor made sure that everyone paid their rent at a special time, and he accounted for everyone. He loved his job and he didn't want to lose it. Because he was well in with the old laird, who was a very old man in his late years. And the factor made sure that everyone paid their rent on time! But as for poor Jack, he was idle. He hadna got a job, he had nothing. All he had was a couple o' pigs, a couple o' goats and an old donkey. And his mother kept a few hens and she sold a few eggs, and that was all. By scrimping and scraping for pennies selling a few eggs, she could keep her and Jack alive. But the factor was always down upon Jack, because Jack was always late paying his rent. Months slipped into months and months slipped into months. Jack couldna afford to pay nae rent. Now this factor was not just a local gentleman. He was a bit of a rogue! And this factor was not just a kind of a nice man, because he was a factor! He was always down upon Jack.

So five or six times in the morning, 'Jack, if you don't pay the rent, you're out! We'll get somebody else in the house,' said the factor. Well, Jack didna want to leave the house because his aging mother needed the old place. And he didna want to shift with her late years. He planned and plotted, tried and scraped and tried to get the wee bits o' work, and put the shillings together to try and get the price o' rent. But try as hard as he could, he could not afford it. So he sat one evening and he planned an idea.

He said, 'Mother, we'll never pay the rent.'

She says, 'Jack, we'll have to leave this place because we cannae afford it.'

'Well,' Jack said, 'Mother, we'll have to think of something.' So he sat and he thought, and being Jack . . . he said, 'Mother, how much money have we got?'

She says, 'Jack, all the money we have in the world between you and me, I've saved and scraped and scrived, is two half-sovereigns.'

'Oh,' says Jack, 'two half-sovereigns. Well, let me see . . . hmmm . . . well, Mother,' he said, 'something's got to be done. Mother, would you gie me the two half-sovereigns? And maybe I'll help to pay the rent.'

'Well,' she says, 'laddie, ye're welcome tae it.'

Now Jack had an old donkey that wandered about the place where he lived. It would eat anything—bits of cloth, bits of anything it found, thistles and bushes and any thorns, it would eat anything this old donkey. So Jack got the two half-sovereigns from his mother, and he looked at them. He looked at the old donkey eating the whin bushes and bits o' rags and bits o' paper and things that was blowin about the place.

'Aha,' says Jack, 'I think I've got an idea how to solve my problem.' Noo in the barn he always had a wee puckle corn, 'cause he grew a wee puckle corn. And he gathered all the wee bits o' corn together, he got some water and he mixed it up. And he went oot, he brought in the old donkey. Now this old donkey had been browsing round the bushes. And because it couldna get much to eat it was very hungry. Jack mixed the two gold half-sovereigns in among the corn and the wee puckle water. He put it in a wee basin, and he fed it to the donkey. And the poor old donkey being so hungry it gobbled the corn as quick as it could, never took time to chew it. It licked up the basin, two half-sovereigns and all. 'Aha,' says Jack, 'that's it!' Noo it happened that that day was market day in the village. So Jack said, 'Mother, I'm takin the donkey to the market the day, I'm gaunna sell it.'

'Ah well, Jack,' she said, 'it's gettin kind o' old, it's no worth very much onyway. Can you get what you can for it? Buy me a wee bit tobacco for my pipe if you get ony money for it.'

'Well,' Jack says, 'I'm sellin it today.' So off he went to the village with the donkey. All the people were gathered round the market. So he took the donkey very gently, never made it walk very hard, just took it gently. So when he landed in the market there were farmers selling hens and ponies and donkeys and everything they could sell. But Jack got out in the market square!

'Ladies and gentlemen!' he cried. Everybody looked at Jack with an old donkey. 'Come you all around me! I have the most fantastic donkey in the world!' But who would be there at that very moment looking for Jack but the factor! Now the factor himself was a bit of a rogue. And he saw Jack with the donkey.

He said, 'If he sells the donkey for money,' thought the factor, 'whatever he gets for it it's for me! Pay the rent. And I'll make sure I'll get it.'

So people began to gather up and Jack's standin with this stick, 'Ladies and gentlemen, you never saw nothing like this. This donkey can drop gold in its dung—once it shites, it'll drop gold! This is a gold donkey, this donkey is loaded with gold. Anyone'll buy it—who'll buy it at the best price?' And he pulled the donkey and he gied the donkey a couple o' welts wi his stick, you see! The donkey had been walkin slow and eatin all the meat that Jack had gien it, all the corn. People began to gather round, this was a pantomime, this was funny. Farmers and people and stallmen all gathered round Jack, you see! And the first in the line was the factor. And Jack beat the donkey, and the donkey lifted its tail, put a big thploosh on the street.

Jack said, 'Watch this, gentlemen! Ladies, children, everybody watch this!' And he went over and he scattered it with his foot. 'Come everybody and look!'

The first person to come was the factor. There in the donkey's dung—two gold half-sovereigns. The people stared in amazement.

One man says, 'I'll take it!'

Another man says, 'I'll buy it!'

Another man says, 'I'll buy it!'

Farmer says, 'I'll buy it!'

'Just a moment,' said the factor. 'Just a moment! I'll have it! How much you want for it, Jack?'

'Well,' Jack says, 'eh, seein as I'll have to sell it and eh, I would think about fifty sovereigns! Fifty gold sovereigns.'

'Done!' says the factor. 'I'll buy it.' And he counted out fifty gold sovereigns in Jack's hand. 'Now,' he said, 'Jack, I'm payin you for this and tomorrow I'm comin for the rent money. Now you have it. I'm no takin it off ye, but tomorrow I'm comin for the rent money.'

Jack said, 'You'll get your rent money, don't worry about it.' He put the fifty gold sovereigns in his pocket, walked into the bar, had a good drink. Then he bought his mother some tobacco, some messages and he walked his way home. When he cam back he said, 'Mother, I sold the donkey.'

She said, 'How did you get on, Jack? Who did you sell it tae?'

He said, 'I sold it to the factor.'

She said, 'You sellt it to the factor? How much did you get for it frae the factor?'

He said, 'Fifty sovereigns.'

But she says, 'Jack, that donkey wasna worth fifty sovereigns!'

'Ah but, Mother,' he said, 'it was worth it to the factor! But I'll tell ye, Mother, there'll probably be a wee bit trouble over this. But pay nae heed! But everything'll come oot to the best anyhow.' But we're leavin Jack for the moment . . .

The factor takes his donkey. He is proud o' this, oho, he's real happy about this! Hurries back to his wife and he tells his wife, 'I bought a donkey today that can shit gold. Come oot and see this! Ye've nae idea!' He took it oot wi a stick, and he beat the donkey and he beat the donkey and the poor donkey shit and it shit until there were not a grain left in its stomach. But nothing. 'Aha,' says the factor, 'Jack played a dirty trick on me. He disna pay his rent. I'm gaunna kill him! Wife,' he said, 'I'm gaunna kill Jack.' She kent who Jack was.

Jack knew what was gaunna happen. So the next day was a beautiful sunny day and he says tae his mother, 'Mother, you're probably gettin a visitor today come lookin for me.'

'What do ye mean, laddie?' she says.

He said, 'The factor.' So he told his mother the story.

'Oh Jack,' she said, 'ye're a foolish laddie. That factor's wild—he'll kill ye. He'll murder ye! Ye should never have done that.'

'Well, Mother,' he says, 'it's done noo, the're nothing we can dae about it. Dinnae worry, I'm Jack! Everything'll work oot for the best!' Noo what Jack had in a box was two rabbits. Jack liked to keep rabbits. Two brown wild rabbits in a box. 'Mother,' he said, 'I ken fine it'll no be long before the factor comes back here lookin fir me. Noo I'm gaun awa fir a wee walk inta the wood tae hide mysel and I'll take ane o' the rabbits wi me.'

65

She says, 'Laddie, what dae ye want tae take a rabbit wi ye fir?'

'Well,' he says, 'I'll tell ye, Mother. When the factor comes lookin fir me you tell him "I'm awa in the wood". And tak that other rabbit oot o' the box and let it go, and tell the rabbit to "go and bring me back". Tell the rabbit to "go and find me"!'

'That's funny,' she said, 'the rabbit'll no find you, Jack, in the worl—it'll run awa!'

'No matter, Mother,' he said, 'if it runs awa or no! I have the other one. Dinnae worry about it. Just dae what I'm tellin ye tae dae.'

So Jack walked away wi the wee brown rabbit under his arm. The other one was in the box. But Jack had only gane in the wood for a wee while when doon from the toon comes the factor! And he's in a ragin mood!

Up to the house he comes, knocks on the door. He says, 'Auld wumman, is your son in?'

She says, 'Dae ye mean Jack?'

'Aye,' he says, 'him, I want him right noo! I'm gaunna kill him. Sellt me a donkey s'posed tae shit gold! Couldna shit nothing! Robbed me, took aa my money. I'm gaunna kill him! Where is he?'

She said, 'He's away in the wood.'

'Oh well,' he said, 'he's away in the wood. When will he be back?'

'Oh,' she said, 'God knows when he'll be back!'

'Well,' he said, 'I want him right noo!'

'Well,' she said, 'just a minute, mister. Dinnae worry yourself. Wait and I'll send this wee rabbit fir him.'

He says, 'What?'

She says, 'Wait and I'll send this wee rabbit fir him, this rabbit'll go for him. This is Jack's favourite rabbit. And this rabbit, maister, can do onything!' So Jack's mother went to the box, she lifted the wee brown rabbit oot the box, she took it oot. She says, 'Go and tell Jack that there's somebody wants tae see him,' and she let the wee rabbit go. And the wee rabbit was glad to get free. It went away hoppin through the wood.

The factor said, 'I don't believe this, I don't believe this. This is another trick. This is another trick!'

'No,' she said, 'this is nae trick. Jist wait, just a minute. Can I mak ye a cup o' tea?'

'No, I'm no wantin nae tea. I want that son o' yirs, I'm gaunna kill him!'

But lo and behold within a few minutes back comes Jack, the wee brown rabbit under his oxter. And he went ower to the box and he put the rabbit—'Go in there,' he said, 'and thank you very much for finding me!'

The factor said, 'Is that really true? Did it come to the wood and get ye?'

'Aye,' says Jack. 'That rabbit, see that rabbit? That rabbit can do anything. That rabbit can do anything, it'll go, send it for messages! It's better than a carrier pigeon!'

'Well,' the factor says, 'I never seen the like o' that. Look, Jack, let me . . . you forget about our quarrels. You cheated me already with the fifty gold sovereigns for the donkey. I know there was nothing in the donkey. But if you gie me that rabbit, we'll call it quits.'

'Ah well,' Jack said, 'I hate tae part wi it, it's an awfa clever rabbit that. And I've had it a long time and it'll do anything! I can send that rabbit to the shop, I can send that rabbit anywhere. It disna matter what you want to do, that rabbit'll dae it for ye.'

'Well, look, Jack,' he said, 'we'll call it quits if you gie me that rabbit! I'll no bother you any mair.'

'Ah well,' Jack says, 'seein ye're bein like that, ye can have it—tak the rabbit!'

So the factor takes the rabbit and away back he goes. He's got the most fantastic rabbit in the world, see! Takes it home, tells his wife. Brags tae everybody in the village, he's got the most fantastic rabbit in the world. Invites all

67

his friends tae his hoose to see this rabbit. Noo the factor had a brother who lived about half a mile down the road. And they all gathered together for to have a party, drinkin party. So he said, 'If youse no believe me, just come in.' So he took them all, gied them all a drink in the hoose. And he said, 'Wait ti ye see this, I've got the cleverest rabbit in the world!' He said, 'We're all gaunna have a drink and a ceilidh tonight. So I never invited my brother because I want to show you this. See what I've got here, a rabbit!' He takes the rabbit. He says, 'Look, rabbit, you gae doon to my brother doon the road and tell my brother that we're havin a ceilidh, and come back here tae the ceilidh!'

People were starin—'A rabbit couldna go to your brother for a ceilidh!'

'Just you wait and see!'

'Rabbit couldna go to your brother's and bring him back for a ceilidh!' says the folk.

He says, 'Just you wait!' He tells the rabbit, 'Right, rabbit, on you go! Don't be long noo, hurry up!'

Wee rabbit went hoppin away among the grass. Ah, it's gone! They waited and they waited and they drank and they sang, and they waited and they sang. They waited and they sang till midnight. No signs o' the rabbit, no signs o' his brother. But then the factor realises Jack has made a fool o' him again.

He said, 'This time I'm gaunna kill him real dead. He's gaunna be murdered! I'm takin no more excuses.'

But meanwhile Jack's back with his mother and he tells her, 'Mother, the factor'll be back again, and God help us!'

'Jack,' she said, 'ye're really gettin yirsel in big trouble. Look, the're naething good gaunna come oot o' this. Whaur is it leadin tae?'

Jack said, 'Dinnae worry!'

She said, 'You've never paid the rent. We'll be flung oot o' this hoose, we've nae whaur tae gang. And ye're aggravatin the man, ye're makin things worse!'

68

'Never mind, Mother,' he said. 'Just a minute!' But what Jack had in the shed was a wee piglet, half grown pig. He went oot to the shed. He had a big knife, about that size. And he cut the pig's throat. Killed it and he gutted it. He took the pig's bladder, and he collected all the pig's blood that he could get and he put it in the pig's bladder. And he tied a wee knot on it. Raw blood. He says, 'Mother, I'm tellin ye, he'll no be long noo! He'll be back in a wee minute. Put this in below your peenie, in alow your apron!' Now Jack's old mother wore an apron.

But she said, 'Laddie, what do ye want me tae put that cauld thing in alow my apron for?'

'Mother, you do what I'm tellin you,' he said. 'Look, if you want this hoose and you want yir rent paid, you do what I'm tellin ye.' So after he convinced his auld mother, she took the bladder full o' pig's blood and she shoved it under her apron in the front of her belly. 'Noo,' he said, 'pull your frock down over it and keep it there.' And he sat doon. But they hadna sat for a few minutes but down comes the factor once again. And he's furious!

He says, 'This time—Jack, ye've done it this time! You gied me a rabbit, a stupid brown rabbit. It was ignorant, it could do nothing. And you tellt me that rabbit was clever! This time, Jack,' he said, 'you're finished. You're finished for ever! I'm gaunna kill you dead this night!'

'But just a minute,' Jack says. 'Mebbe it wasna the rabbit's fault. Mebbe it was your fault. I've been fair wi you,' he says, 'fair wi you. But look, I'll tell ye what I'll dae wi you. I'll give you something more special than the donkey, than the rabbit.'

'What would that be?' said the factor.

And Jack took oot the big knife. He says, 'This. This knife.' He said, 'Ye see this knife, factor? This is the most important knife in the world. Because this can kill folk and mak them better!'

Factor says, 'Jack, I'm havin no more o' this noo. No more

o' it. You've done me twice already! I want the rent money. And after I get the rent money, I'm gaunna kill ye!'

Jack says, 'Noo just hold it a minute. Just watch this!' He says, 'Mother, gie me ower my pipe!' Jack smoked a pipe.

She says, 'Get yir ain pipe.'

He says, 'Mother, I tellt ye tae give me my pipe.'

She says, 'Get yir ain pipe! I'm no needed tae fill yir pipe for ye.'

'Mother,' he said, 'I'm giein ye one more chance. Give me my pipe!'

She said, 'Get yir ain pipe!'

He says, 'Ye'll no gie me my pipe?'

'No!' she said, 'I wouldna gie ye yir pipe!'

He says, 'Factor, watch this!' And he walks over to his mother's belly, and he jabs the knife intae her. 'Mebbe that'll get you the pipe!' And all the blood fell doon oot o' the pig's bladder, spread across the floor.

And the factor stood back and he said, 'Ye killed yir mother! Ye killed yir mother.'

'No,' Jack said, 'I never killed my mother. Never killed my mother, no with this knife!' And there was the old woman's blood lyin runnin on the floor—from the pig's bladder. And Jack went ower and he took the knife and he held it in front of his mother's face and he touched her forehead with it, and he says, 'Are ye all right, Mother? Come on, Mother, get up, Mother!'

And the old woman got up, she says, 'All right, all right, laddie, I'll get ye yir pipe!' And she cleaned all the blood from the front o' her dress.

The factor stood in amazement. He says, 'Jack, that is a really fantastic knife! I've never seen nothing like that in all my life!' He said, 'Look, I'll make a promise wi ye. I'll give ye this hoose free fir the rest o' yir days, I'll never ask you for rent again as long as you live, if you give me that knife.'

'No,' Jack said, 'I couldna give ye it. I couldna give you that knife, factor. It disna matter what you do for me, I couldna give you that.' He says, 'This is the most magic knife in the worl! I can kill a pig wi this knife and mak it come living again. I can kill a human being wi this knife and mak it come livin again. I can do anything wi this knife.'

Factor said, 'Jack, look, please for my sake, gie me the knife. I'll never bother ye again! I swear.'

'All right,' says Jack, 'you can have the knife. But I'm payin you no more rent as long as I live in this hoose.'

'I swear,' says the factor, 'I'll never bother you again if you give me that knife!' Big dagger that length!

Jack says, 'All right, there ye are then.' So him and the factor shook hands, and off the factor went.

Factor took it in his belt. He had the finest magic knife in the world. He was gaunna have some fun with his friends. He could kill them all and bring them livin again! He could kill his ain wife and bring her livin again! He was gaunna have a ceilidh, he was gaunna gather all the people in the village together. He was the factor, he could do anything. Well with this knife he could dae anything. So that night he invited everybody to come up tae his house, he was gaunna have a big ceilidh. He was going to show them something special, something real special! So naturally, the people o' the village cam to the factor's hoose. Brought them in, gied them all a good drink, sat them all round.

'Now,' he said, 'I've got a special treat for you tonight. I'm gaunna show youse something you never saw in all your life.' So they were all sittin doon. And the wife was a-givin them all drinks. He says, 'Wife, fill my pipe!'

She says, 'What do ye mean, fill yir pipe? Fill yir ain pipe,' she said, 'I'm too busy!'

He said, 'Wife, fill my pipe I told you!'

She looked up and she said, 'What do ye mean? You never asked me to fill yir pipe before.'

'Well,' he said, 'fill it now! I'm warnin ye, fill it to me right now.'

She says, 'Go and fill yir ain pipe!'

71

He says, 'Ye wouldna fill my pipe would ye? Now,' he says, 'watch this!' And everybody stared.

And then he took the knife and he stuck it into his wife's belly. Right in her stomach. And the poor woman fell to the floor. Dead. And the people rushed oot, reported him to the police. The factor stood there, and he says, 'Dear, dear, dear, my poor wife!' And he tried his best to revive her, but it was too late. She was gone. And he took the knife and he said, 'If only I had time . . . Jack done it again. But,' he says, 'this time I'll get him!'

And he got up and he had his knife in his hand, when in the door comes two policemen. The people in the village had reported the factor had murdered his wife. And he was arrested, he was thrown in prison. The factor was hung for the murder of his wife. For Jack and his old mother, they lived in that hoose for the rest of their life, and Jack never paid any more rent!

JACK AND THE POTS

This is a wee story my father tellt me long long ago, aye, when I was young afore I went to school. See, the great thing about traveller stories at one time, the travellers liked the simple stories. Ye'll ay notice whenever ye get travellers aboot tellin ye a story, every one'll ay have a story about Daft Sandy or Simple Jack or Jack and his Mother because they thought a lot o' the simpleton, the underdog that wasna sae soft as that. Because in a way they were referrin to theirsels, ye see. Oh, these stories are gettin told as much noo as ever they was, aye. Folk there tells them to their sons and their daughters and that when they're weans.

Jack and Sandy were two brothers. When their father died they were very young and they stayed with their mother. But the years passed by and Sandy was always the strongest, and he was always bigger than Jack. Jack was always the weak one. And he made Jack do everything that was needed to be done. But the years passed by, Jack begint to grow up and he begint to get a wee bit stronger than Sandy. But Sandy still remained the boss. He was the biggest one and the oldest one and what he said had to be done.

One day Sandy took a thocht to hissel, 'Look Mother,' he said, 'the're no much here now that me and Jack hes growed up, and aa you've got about yir wee place is jist enough to keep yirsel. I think the best thing I can dae,' he says, 'is go awa and have a wander through the country and look fir a

73

bit job to mysel, an' see if I can get some money tae mysel instead o' bidin wi you, fir aa the work you've got here on this wee croft, Jack can dae it.'

'Ah no,' says Jack. 'Look, ever since I've been wee you ordered me, and made me dae everything roon aboot this place. And noo you're gaunna slip awa on yir own through the country and lea me here wi my mother! Well,' he said, 'that's no gaunna dae! I'm goin wi ye.'

'You cannae come wi me, ye're far too wee to come wi me,' he said. 'I cannae take care o' mysel, never mind take care o' you!'

'Well,' he says, 'I'm still gaun wi ye.'

But they hemmed, they hawed and they argued, and they argued and bargued about it. But anyway, Sandy turned around, he said, 'Look, Jack, if you're comin wi me, there's only one thing for it; you'll dae what I tell ye! It makes no difference what it is, you'll dae it. Or I'll mak ye dae it!' He says, 'Every time we need onything tae eat, you'll go to the hooses and the fairms,' he said, 'and ye'll ask it, ye'll ask fir work and ye'll ask fir everything that's tae be etten by me and you. That's the way ye're gaunnae get it to happen.'

'All right,' says Jack, 'I've been used daein it all my days, I willna take no ill wi it.' But away they set, the two of them. Their mother made them a wee bannock and a wee bit collop and they said good-bye to their mother, and away they went on the road.

But they travelled . . . in these days the places and villages and toons were far atween each other. So they travelled on and on and on and here and there, but ah-h-h-h, Jack begint to get fed up with travelling. Every hoose that he cam tae, Sandy would sit at the road-end, 'Go up to that farm, Jack, and ask fir work!'

Jack had to go and ask fir work. 'No-o,' the man says. 'Nae work here,' he says, 'no much work for myself.'

'If yese dinnae get work, ask for something to eat,' Sandy would say.

Right, Jack goes, asks for something to eat. But the're some days the farmers put the dogs on him, chased him to the road. Every time that Jack cam back wantin onything, Sandy gied him a beatin, kicked him and hit him, welted him. Poor Jack's in an awfa state. And whenever Jack got onything on a farm, a good bit meat to eat or anything, can o' milk or something to drink, Sandy took the biggest share and poor Jack was left with very very little.

But Jack begint to get this idea into his heid. He said tae hissel, 'Look, I'd be better mysel—if I've got to go and ask for enough to eat to keep mysel alive along the road and ask for work—and he sits at the road-end daein nothing, I'd be better on my own. But I cannae get awa, because he'll no let me go, get awa fae him.'

But he cam doon onyway, and this woman had nae work, but she gied him a good peck o' scones and a lump o' cheese. So as usual when Jack cam doon with the scones and the cheese and the milk that the woman gied him on the farm, Sandy commanded it. And he sat and he ate the maist o' it and he gied Jack one sip o' milk and one wee bit o' cheese and a wee toy bit o' scone.

'That's enough for you,' he said to Jack, 'you dinnae need as much as me. I suppose you got a lot mair in the hoose and you ett it on the road doon.'

'No me,' says Jack, 'that was all I got, that's all the woman gied me.'

'Well,' says Sandy, 'the next hoose ye gang to make sure you get mair because I'm feelin awfa hungry. That's no gaunnae do me no guid!'

And poor Jack he's as waik as water. He never got a hauf as much as Sandy got. So they set on, and on they go. But they travelled and they travelled and they travelled for miles and miles and miles ower this hill. But not a hoose, not a single hoose in sight. Sandy started complainin to Jack worst way he could.

Jack says, 'I cannae help it.'

75

'Look,' he said, 'the next farm you come to, you'd better get me something to eat,' he said, 'or as low as my father, I'm gaunnae kill ye. Only for you comin wi me onyway . . .'

Jack said, 'If I hadna come wi ye, ye'd be deid wi hunger long ago. What did you do for yirsel since we left wir mother's? Nothing!'

'Ach,' said Sandy, 'I'd be better athoot ye!'

'No,' says Jack, 'you couldna do withoot me! Only for me you'd be gotten deid with hunger.' But they argued and bargued and they travelled on, they travelled. They were as waik as water. They couldna get a bite. They travelled all that day until the next. But the middle o' the next day they seen the first hoose. They looked away doon in the hollow, oh, half a mile doon the old cart road—there's a farm.

'Go on,' says Sandy, 'gae doon to that farm!'

Jack says, 'It's a lang road doon, I'm that waik I cannae hardly travel.'

'Get doon,' he says, 'afore I kick ye doon!'

'I'm gaun doon,' said Jack, 'and if I get onything I hope in God it may be yir last, the last ye'll ever eat!' he said to hissel so's Sandy couldna hear him. The folk were workin at the harvest, it was the harvest time. Away goes poor Jack. Down he goes. He travelled, oh, he must hae travelled aboot half a mile off the main road doon this old coorse road to the farm. He landed at the farm. Up to the door. Knocked at the door. Not a soul. Rung the old fashioned bell—not a soul. Roond the back o' the steadings. Oh, the lovely smell o' cookin would choke ye! It was goin for him, smell, beautiful smell comin from the kitchen. He gaes roond to the back o' the kitchen. Knocks, pulls the bell. Not a soul. He keeks into the kitchen—there's two great big pots sittin.

'Tsst,' he says tae hissel, 'maybe it's tatties. I dinnae see a soul aboot. It's maybe a pot o' tatties.' He walks in and he lifts the lid off the pot; beautiful pot o' dry Golden Wonder tatties jist ready—poored and everything, sittin dry as meal. And he lifts the lid o' the other pot, it was thon old fashioned metal

76

pots in these days, ye know! It was full o' beautiful boiled beef. 'Well upon my soul,' says Jack, 'suppose I get the jail or suppose I get killt, I'm gaunnae have a bit o' this.' Quick as he could he swallowed two hot tatties and then he ate a lump o' this beef. He says, 'I have to tak something back to him on the road or he'll kill me deid.' But he searched the hoose for somethin to put it in, but there was nothing. 'Tsst, ach tae hell with it!' he said. He took the two pots ane in each hand. And away he goes, pot in each hand up the road. He travels up, never seen a soul about the place.

But unkenned tae him, through the wood aroond the back o' the farm the woman had made the dinner and the men was oot cuttin corn with scythes. And she'd walked doon the wee pad tae shout tae the men tae come for their dinner. Two brothers, wicked farm brothers they were. And thes two brothers were about six foot apiece. The woman went doon to shout them for their dinner, ye see.

But anyway, we'll go up the lead, the story with Jack first. Jack carries up to the main road a pot in each hand. Sandy sees him comin, wouldna event rise and meet him. He sat till he cam up.

'What hae you got?' he said.

'Oh wheesht!' he says.

He said, 'Did ye ask for work?'

'Tsst, work,' he said, 'bings o' work! Folk's needin all the men they can get fir the harvest.'

He said, 'Did ye ask for boots or claes or something to wear?'

'Well,' he said, 'tae tell ye the God's truth, the woman said efter you come back, efter thon, that she's got some claes and boots belangin tae her brothers that they're no needin, that ye can get them.'

'What hae you got in the pots?'

'Tatties,' he said, 'and beef.'

Oh, lifted the lid off the pot, Sandy said, 'Don't you touch it till I get my share first! Pro'bly,' he said, 'you must hae ate the lot o' it on the road up onyway.' Oh, he was wicked tae him.

Poor Jack had tae sit and watch him. Sandy ate the best he could, till he left nane but the wee smurach o' tatties at the bottom o' the pot. The wee bits o' fat beef that was left, he says, 'There, you can have that.'

Poor Jack had to pick awa in the pots. Never said a word. 'Man,' Jack says, 'that's beautiful claes that that woman hes doon there.'

'What?' says Sandy.

He said, 'She flung oot some beautiful claes but I couldna carry them.'

'Would they fit me?' says Sandy. 'I'm badly needin something, I'm in rags.'

'Tsst, jist about your fit,' says Jack. 'They'll jist fit ye to a tee.'

'Ah well,' he said, 'seein the're something good goin, and the're a job . . .'

Jack had tellt him, 'He only wants ae body. He's no wantin two fir the harvest, only ae man. And they'll gie him a good job and a place tae stay in the bothy.'

'Ah well,' Sandy said, 'that's jist the job for me. You can carry on, carry on and look for a job tae yirsel. I'm gettin kind o' fed up wi ye onyway.' Jack's heart begint tae beat, ye ken, he was glad tae get rid o' him. Sandy was real bad to him. 'And,' Sandy said, 'tae mak things better, I'll maybe bide in the bothy for a while and get that old claes and a few pound to mysel. And I'll maybe go on to the toon, and settle doon here and go back and see my old mother sometime. Look, you better get on, and dinnae come about me. Dinnae you come aboot me,' he said, 'I'm no wantin tae even ken you ataa!'

'All right,' says Jack, 'if that's the way you want it. Nae harm done. Is that the thanks I get fir bein so good tae you?'

'Aye bein good to you!' Sandy said. 'What do ye mean?

Didna I rear ye up aa the days sin yir faither de'it? And lookin efter ye, and workin hard tae bring ye up?'

'Aye,' said Jack, 'I ken, ye jist made me a slave aa the days o' my life!'

'But onyway, I'm no gaunnae argue the point aboot it, I'll tak the job. And I'll go back wi the pots.'

'You dae that,' says Jack. 'I'm that tired, I cannae hardly walk doon there.'

'Oh, you're no goin onyway!' says Sandy. 'I'm gettin the job and I'm gettin the claes and I'm gaun back wi the pots to the farm.'

'Right,' says Jack, 'you dae that and I'll wait.'

'Now ye mightna wait on me,' he said, 'because I'll no be back if I get the job. If the man gives me a job and place to stay on the farm I'll no be back.'

'Oh,' says Jack tae his ainsel, 'I jan ye'll no be back richt enough!' But Jack sits onyway, he's no hungry because he's had a good feed, two good bits oot the pot before he cam up. He says tae hissel, 'I'll wait till I hear the roars, and then I'll go. And guid luck tae him!'

But onyway, Sandy goes away with a pot in each hand whistlin doon the road, farm road.

But the farmer woman cam back. The men sat doon to the table. She set the table. And roond to the kitchen. Two pots was gone. The woman ran roond to her man and her man's brother. And thes two men's dyin with waikness in the field!

He said, 'What's wrong? Did ye burn yirsel or something?'

'No,' she said. 'The pot o' tatties and the pot o' beef's gone!'

'Ah, woman, ye're no wise! Hoo could the pot o' tatties . . . The're nobody aboot here tae tak it,' he said.

She says, 'Come and see fir yirsel.'

The man cam tae the kitchen, searched the kitchen. 'The pot,' he said, 'ye couldna . . .'

She said, 'Look, the two pots is gone! Ye ken the two pots I've got, the same two big enamel pots—they're gone.'

The man searched the hoose. No, the pots was gone. 'Ah,' he said, 'God knows what happened.' But he sat doon the table and he said, 'Mak us a cup o' tea and gie us a bit scone or something, we'll go back oot to the harvest.'

But the kitchen window where the folk was sittin in the sittin room was level with the door goin to the hoose. And it was a beautiful day, the sun was shinin, the man had the window open. Here's Sandy comin whistlin with the two pots, ane in each hand. The farmer looks oot of the window.

He says to his wife, 'Come here! Look, look at that scaldie tramp comin with yir two pots! Did you gie him them?'

'No me,' she said, 'he must hae stole them.'

'Oh, stole them!' says the farmer. 'Just a minute . . .'

Sandy knocks at the door. Oot comes the farmer. Sandy said, 'Thank you very much sir, and thank your lady very much. We sure enjoyed that tatties and that beef,' he said. 'It was jist what we were needin.'

'Oh,' said the farmer, 'you enjoyed it, did you? Hmm-mm. Whaur do ye come fae?'

'Oh,' he said, 'I cam a long way—I'm lookin fir work. And my young brother was doon and he tellt me that ye gied him that pot o' tatties and the pot o' beef and you would hae a job fir me at the harvest. And a change o' clean claes,' he said, 'and a place to stay.'

'Aye,' said the farmer, 'I've got that for you aa right. Very thing I have for you. Gae in there tae that shed and,' he says, 'take yir boots off and yir claes off and I'll gang in and get the wife tae raik oot some clean claes tae you. Ye're kind o' raggie, I dinnae want ye in my hoose the way ye're kind o' rags on ye.'

'Good,' says Sandy, 'I'm a good worker, I'll work.'

'Oh,' says the farmer, 'ye'll work aa right! Ye'll work,' he says, 'I guarantee it.' He gaes in tae his brother, he tells his brother the story. He said, 'He stole the two pots and

80

he ate the lot. Noo he wants,' he said, 'he wants a job and a place tae stay.' Oh, he was the oldest brother tae. These were rough wicked farmers they were. So they explained to the woman. 'But dinnae say a word,' says the man, 'dinnae say a word! He's in the shed and we're supposed to bring claes up.'

'I'll bring claes oot tae him,' says the youngest brother. 'Just a minute . . .' He goes to the stable and he takes doon from the stable a horse whip. And he goes. When he goes into the shed Sandy's standin nothing but the trousers on his bare body and his bare feet. Jist the troosers.

He said, 'Did ye bring . . .'

'Aye, I brang ye the clothes,' said the farmer. And he fell tae him with his whip. And he laid on him and he laid on him, he gied him the biggest beatin in the worl with this whip! And the yowls and screams wis comin—Jack's sittin in the road away a good bit frae the farm and he hears the screams and the squeals o' Sandy in the stable—where the two farmer brothers, ane layin on with the whip and ane flingin handfuls o' salt on to him! Till they gied him the wildest beatin in the worl wi his bare feet.

'Noo,' said the farmer, 'come with me! Wi yir bare feet!' And they tak him to the field. Where all the harvest was lyin cut, ye ken, they cut the corn sheaths lang ago wi a binder and left them in rows. And then ye had to pick 'em and stook 'em in fours together to mak wee stooks. One farmer took one whip and he stood at the top o' the field. And the other farmer stood at the bottom o' the field wi the other whip. 'Noo,' he said to Sandy, 'you gae up and doon that field and don't stop! If we ever see ye stoppin till the hale field is stooked'—oh, about five acre o' corn, and the sheafs o' corn jist lies in rows—they put him to the field. And poor Sandy's up and doon, and up and doon, stookin and every fear o' stoppin. The sweat was breakin off him, and wi the beatin he got with his bare feet among the stubble o' the corn, they worked him

81

the hale fearin day! When night was comin they took him up to the farm.

'Now,' says the farmer, 'ye see that road ye cam doon? Get up it! As fast as ye can,' and he flung his auld boots after him. He says, 'Never show yir face again back tae this farm as long as you live!' after Sandy worked fir a whole fearin day and stooked the hale five acre o' corn.

Jack heard the screams and murder and went away, travelled on and on and on, oh, looking back in case Sandy would catch him again. But Sandy never catcht him. But Jack cam to this crossroads and he cut away to the left, he went away to another road and up to this wee farm. He got a job with an old man and woman. He worked away for years with the old man and woman, and he married the old woman's daughter. He lived happy ever after fir the rest of his days. But what happened to Sandy, God only kens. Naebody never heard another word about him!

THE BLACK THIEF OF SLANE

The travellers really loved Jack tales. You see, when fathers
were telling weans their stories, they wanted to get it through
to them, especially traveller men telling it to their wee laddies
roond the fire, *they* could be Jack. Like weans in your culture
when they grow up, 'I want to be a policeman, I want to be a
train driver, I want to be a pilot.' Weans listening to the story
want to grow up to be like Jack. They didna want to be feart,
they didna want to be thieves, they wanted to be cleverer than
each other. Oh yes, *every* wean listened—Jack tales werenae
made for laddies—there's nae such thing! In most tales ye
had Jack, ye had his mother, his auntie, the henwife, ye
had the king, the queen and the princess in many stories,
ye had the miller or the old woman. It wasnae only about
Jack . . .

For years the old king had ruled the land with an iron hand.
He'd been a hard king on his subjects. Some people loved
him and some people hated him. He had been a great warrior
king at one time, and a great soldier and a great hunter.
But now he was gettin old . . . in fact he was sick. The
king had tooken some kind o' strange sickness that no one
could help him with. And word had spread far and wide,
and they offered a large reward for anyone who would
come and help the king. Some people were pleased about
this, some people were sad, because some loved and some
hated him. So quacks and wisemen came from all parts of

the country tryin to help, but no one could. The king lay in bed with this strange sickness. Nothing would make him happy, nothing would make him healthy, nothing would make him feel well. Till one day an old woman walked up the steps of the palace with a little basket on her arm.

Immediately she was stopped wi the guards at the front of the palace, because they guarded the palace well. And one of them said, 'Where are ye goin old beggar woman?'

She says, 'Indeed, son, I'm not a beggar.'

'Well,' he said, 'what are ye, are ye a witch or something?'

'No,' she said, 'I'm not a witch.'

He said, 'Well, what do you want?'

She says, 'I've come to help the king.'

'Oh,' he said, 'ye've come to help the king, have ye?' He was head of the guards of the palace.

'Yes,' she said, 'my son, I've come to help the king. And get out of my way and let me see the king!'

So the head guard he was very pleased. And he brought the old woman in to the palace. The first person he brought her to was the queen. Now the queen was a very worried woman because her husband the king was sick, very sick. And she would hae gien her life to anyone who would do the king any good.

And the guard says, 'This is an old woman who has come to help the king.'

Oh, the queen was very excited. 'At last!' she said. She told the guard to go on his way. So the old woman sat down. And she had a wee basket on her arm. The queen says, 'You've come to help my husband the king?'

'Oh yes,' said the old woman, 'I've come to help your husband.' And she said, 'I'd like to see him.'

She said, 'What are ye, a henwife or something?'

'Well,' she said, 'not really. I'm not a henwife.'

She says, 'Are ye . . . a witch or something?' said the queen.

84

'Oh no really,' says the old woman, 'I'm not a witch.' But she says, 'I would like to see the king anyway.'

'I'll lead ye to him,' says the queen.

'Oh no,' says the old woman. 'Just show me where to go, I'll go by myself.'

And she said, 'You don't want me around?'

'No,' says the old woman, 'I don't want you around. I just want to see the king's bedroom!'

So the queen says, 'Through that door there is the king's bedroom.' Beautiful carved door, you know!

So the old woman walked through, and there was the four-poster bed. She closed the door behind her. There lyin on the bed was the king. Very sick. In his dressing gown lyin on the bed. And the old woman cam up, the king was lyin with his face to the door. And the old woman placed the wee basket on the floor by her feet. She took her hand and she placed it on the king's forehead, and she could feel it was very hot and warm. He was really sick. And his eyes opened.

And he said, 'What do you want, old woman?'

She says, 'My sire, I've come to help you.'

King said, 'Help me? Well, woman, I don't think you could help me. You know I'm very ill.'

'*Oh, I can see that,*' says the old woman. '*But I can make you better, you know.*'

'Make me better?' said the king. 'There's no one can do anything for me. Woman, I've been like this for weeks.'

But she says, '*I can help you.*' And the old woman reached in—she had a wee cloth over her basket, and she pulled the wee cloth off—she reached in, and she took out from the basket an apple. She says to the king, '*Take a bite of that, my lord!*' A beautiful rosy apple.

And the king reached up with a feeble hand and he took the apple . . . anything to help him. He took a bite off it very slowly. And he held it in his mouth.

She said, 'Chew it and swallow it!'

85

And the king took a bite and he chewed it and swallowed it. Then, within seconds . . . the king began to feel better. Strangeness came over the king. He sat up in bed. He said, 'Old woman, what is in the apple?'

She says, 'Never mind, my lord. Eat the rest of the apple!'

So the king ate and swallowed the rest of the apple. And he . . . the king felt like he never felt before in his life! He flung his legs over the bed, his dressing gown beside the old woman and he sat on the bed. He said, 'Old woman, you've worked a miracle! Never in my life have I felt like this!.'

'Well,' she says, 'do you feel well?'

'Well!' he said. 'I feel better than I ever . . . Woman, I'm gaunna give you the best reward that you ever had in yir life! Where do you come from?'

She says, 'Never mind, my lord, where I come from! Do you feel well? Do you feel good?'

'Good?' he said. 'I never felt like this in all my life.'

'Well,' she says, 'my lord, now I have done something for you—will you do something for me?'

'Woman, anything in my power! Anything in my power,' he says, 'if I possess it, you can have it! Gold, money? Reward?'

'No, my sire, I need none of your gold. I need none of your reward.' She said, 'All I ask of you is a little favour.'

'Oh, just name it! And,' he said, 'I'll do anything within my power.'

'Well,' she said, 'you see, it's my son.'

He said, 'What about your son?'

'My son,' she said, 'is a prisoner.'

'A prisoner?' he said. 'I'll set him free! Is he in jail, is he in a dungeon or something like that? I'll have him free if it's within my power in seconds!'

She says, 'My son is a prisoner with The Black Thief of Slane!'

Oh, the king rubbed his head. 'Tsst, well,' he said, 'you put me in a very terrible position. You see, The Black Thief of Slane is the most powerful magician in all the land, my dear.'

She says, 'That I know well.'

He said, 'Do ye know that The Black Thief of Slane can come and take the ring from my finger and I wouldn't even know he'd done it? He could take my queen from me, he could take anything I own, and I wouldn't even know he'd done it. I can't send my soldiers into his land. In fact, the only thing I have between The Black Thief of Slane and me—we built a pact between us—that I keep out of his territory and he keeps out of mine. Now,' he said, 'I know he has a silver mine on his land. I know that perfectly well. In fact, many of my soldiers 's been tooken a prisoner with The Black Thief of Slane. And, if that's where yir son is, my dear, there's little I can do. It's the peril of my life to interfere with The Black Thief of Slane!' he said. 'You made me well. I appreciate it, but I think there's nothing I can do to help you.'

'Well,' she says, 'the effect of the apple will soon wear off.'

'Oh no,' he says, 'please no!'

And she put her hand in her basket, and she brought out another two. Beautiful apples. She said, '*Look, my lord, that has the power of eternal life.*' And she held them in her hand. The king's eyes blazed when he saw these apples.

He said, 'Woman, I could take them from you!' He got kind of upset. He said, 'I could take them and use them.'

She said, 'You could, my lord. But they wouldn't do you any good. They would only turn to dust.'

And the king knew he was up against someone he could do nothing with. So he raiked his brains for a solution.

And she said, 'Are you gaunnae help me, my lord?'

'Well,' he said, 'woman, let me think, let me think for a moment, let me think.' And then . . . a smile came across his face and he said, 'Well, maybe I could. Now I'm not promisin. But I have a friend,' he said, 'who maybe could help us.'

'My lord, all I'm askin of you is,' she said, 'to get my son rescued from The Black Thief of Slane. *And these two apples are yours,*' she said, '*they bear eternal life. You can keep them as long as you're alive and if you're ever ill or sick or unwell again, use them and they'll give you eternal life. But you must set my son free!*'

The king said, 'I promise ye. Well, I half promise ye. I will find someone who will try and help.'

'Well,' she said, 'that's all I'm askin of ye.' And the old woman picked up her wee basket, and away she went and she was gone.

'Aha,' said the king, 'it's a queer predicament I'm in. But I'll have to call on Jack wonst again. It's the only thing I can do.' So he got up, dressed himself. The queen was overjoyed, everyone was overjoyed to see the king well and fit. The old woman had worked a miracle. The king went to one of his soldiers, he gave orders, 'Take a fast horse, two fast horses! And ye'll ride and find my friend Jack. And bring him before me. Tell him I want to see him!'

So, in the meantime, Jack lived with his mother miles away in the forest cuttin wood for firewood for his mother. And Jack and his mother were very happy. Jack had worked for the king, done many jobs for the king and the king had always paid him handsomely. Jack had no need to work, he was rich. Because he worked for the king often. So Jack and his mother were just sittin havin a wee cup o' tea or a wee bit something to eat, when in through the court o' their little house rode a soldier with a spare horse. And the old woman saw him comin.

She says, 'Jack, that's one o' the king's soldiers.'

'Ah well, Mother,' he says, 'this is it again. This is it again. I suppose it's another job for the king.'

She says, 'Jack, I wonder what it'll be this time. It breaks my heart to see ye goin, because some day you're gaunna go, Jack, and you're no gaunna come back.'

'Ah well, Mother,' he says, 'if that's to be, so be it! But ye know fine, when the king sends for me I have to go!'

So the soldier stopped, jumped off his horse. And he cam up, he said hello to the old woman. He said, 'Jack, I've got a message for ye. The king wants to see ye.'

'Oh, I thought so,' says Jack, 'when I saw ye comin, I thought so.'

'Anyhow,' he says, 'the king wants to see ye as soon as possible. And he sent a spare horse for ye.'

So Jack bade his mother good-bye and he climbed on the spare horse. He and the soldier rode away.

Oh, his old mother sat there an' she said, 'My poor laddie, God knows where he's goin this time, maybe to the end of the world.' Jack always told his mother the stories where he'd been when he came back. And he had many queer adventures in his life. She was wondering where he was going this time.

So anyway, to make a long story short, Jack rode back to the palace and the king was pleased to see him. They sat and talked for a wee while, discussed other things that Jack had done for the king. Jack was always wondering, the king never brought up what he wanted Jack to do. Jack was thinking, what was it going to be this time?

And then the king said, 'Jack my son, I have a problem.'

'Ah well,' Jack said, 'I heard you were ill for a while, you were sick. And I was comin to see you, but I never got around . . .'

'Oh,' he said, 'I'm all right now, Jack, I'm all right now.'

'I was comin to see you, but I never got around to it. I would have come through time,' said Jack.

'Ah well, Jack, thanks to an old friend,' he said, 'I'm perfect now, never felt better in all my life!'

'Well,' Jack said, 'get to the point—what is it this time?'

He said, 'Jack, I have a problem.'

'Well,' Jack said, 'a problem halved 's a problem shared— tell me about it.'

'Jack, I had a visit frae an old woman who made me well. And,' he said, 'for the peril of my life, I don't know, somewhere frae within my kingdom she comes. But I don't know where. And this old woman made me well.' He went up by his bed and he pulled back the bedcover and he took out the two apples. He said, 'Jack, look at that. The're enough power in that to keep me and you alive for the rest of wir life! But,' he said, 'it's up to you.'

Jack said, 'That's queer. In the name o' God, what are ye talkin about?' So the king explained the situation to Jack and told him. Jack had heard o' The Black Thief o' Slane, but Jack wasna worryin. He had never entered The Black Thief o' Slane's territory in his life. For the king had never given him any jobs to go to the Black Thief's territory before.

He says, 'Jack, that old woman has got a son, a big blonde son she told me, a prisoner with the Black Thief o' Slane. And what she wants ye to do is go and rescue him. Jack,' he said, 'look, naebody has never returned from the territory of the Black Thief o' Slane. Nobody, Jack, can return. And this is the job I'm givin you. It's the peril of yir life to go or not to. I'm not forcin you to go, I cannae force ye. And I wouldna ask you only for the sake of my own life and yours. But to lose you, Jack,' he said, 'is like losin my own life. You're like a son to me.'

'Well, my lord,' he said, 'my king . . .' because Jack and the king were good friends, he said, 'there's nothing . . . I can try.'

'Jack,' he said, 'it's up to yirsel. If ye want money and if you want a horse, if you want anything I have, Jack, ye can just ask for it. Ye'll get whatever ye want.'

'Och,' Jack said, 'a good horse would help me.'

So, to make a long story short, Jack next morning after he had dined and wined with the king all night and had a good sleep in the palace, the next morning the guard saddled Jack a fresh horse. Jack bade farewell to the queen, bade farewell to the king, and they watched him disappear in the distance. Jack was gone.

And the king scratched his head, 'I wonder, my dear,' he said, 'will my friend ever come back again to see me? He is goin into dangerous territory.' And Jack was gone.

So Jack didna worry much about this. It was another adventure for him. So he rode on and he rode on, he rode on, travelled for days, slept some nights in the wood because he had plenty bundles with him. Unsaddled his horse every evening, gave it plenty to eat. And he rode and he rode till at last he cam to a river. He went down to the river. It wasna large, but it was a steep flowin river. And he thought to himself, 'I wonder can my horse be able to cross that river? Will I walk it, will I swim it, what way will I go across it?'

And he heard a voice saying, 'Sit on it, of course! The horse'll manage.'

He looked roond, and sitting on a stane was an auld woman with a mutch over her head. And Jack couldna see her face. She was sitting on a stane with a long black dress and a mutch over her head.

She says, 'You've come a long way, haven't ye?'

Jack cam and he said, 'Yes, old woman, I've come a long way.'

And she said, 'I suppose you'll be going to the land of The Black Thief of Slane?'

'Well,' says Jack, 'that's where I'm going.'

'Oh,' she said, 'oh ho! I dare you to cross that river tonight!'

'Well,' Jack said, 'I'll have to. The're a dear friend of mine a prisoner with The Black Thief of Slane. And it's the life of my king and the life of myself, and I have to try and set him free.'

The old woman said, 'Well, well, well . . . I'll help you.' And she opened her dress, she took a stane bottle, a stone bottle from under her dress. She says, 'I like you, young man.'

But Jack looked at her, and her face was covered with

91

a kind of black shawl. He could see that she was an old woman.

And she held it oot with her hand. She says, 'Take this, my son.' It was a long stone bottle. 'Now,' she says, 'do you know anything about The Black Thief of Slane?'

Jack said, 'I've heard the name only. But the rest, I know nothing.'

She says, 'You know The Black Thief of Slane lives i' a castle in the mountains and it's guarded by ravens that never sleep. And the moment ye enter his territory these ravens'll warn him and you'll never even get near the place.'

'Well,' Jack said, 'I have to go just the same.'

She said, 'If you listen to me, and do what I tell you, you'll pro'bly manage. You cross that river tonight when it gets dark,' she says, 'wait till it gets a little darker and cross that river tonight! And get as near to the clift castle as you can.' Then from under her shawl she took a knife, a large shiny knife. And she held it up. She said, 'With this you'll kill your horse!'

'Kill my horse!' says Jack. 'It's no event my horse to kill. It's the king's horse.'

'You'll kill the horse,' she said, 'my son. And you'll spread this bottle over its body tonight. And you shall wait till the ravens come. Now be off with you! I'll be here when you return.' Jack was just about to mount his horse when she says, 'Just a moment, my young man, I've something else to tell you. You've never met The Black Thief of Slane, have you?'

'No,' he says, 'I've never met him, but we will meet before the evening's over.'

'Not this evening,' she said, 'but maybe tomorrow. But remember! He's not such a person as you think he is, though the stories you've heard. He gives every prisoner a chance to fight or to work, to wrastle with him or fight him. And you wouldna have a chance! But he'll challenge you, young man. And remember, when he challenges you, accept! Don't fight him, but wrastle him! And try your best to get a hold of his right toe. And when you get your hand on his right toe, never let it go! Now be off with you.'

Jack thought this was queer i' the world. What kind o' auld woman was this, was this a witch or something? But he remembered what the old woman told him. So he crossed the river in the darkness. It wasna too deep. And he rode and he rode on and he rode on till he saw the shadow of the clifts in the darkness. And then he pulled his horse under the clift. He took the knife and he cut the horse's throat. And the horse fell. He took the bottle, the little stone bottle, and he spread it all over, stuff from the bottle all over the horse's body. There the horse was lyin. And he spread all the stuff over the horse's body. Then he went and hid in the clifts. He waited and he waited. Till daybreak.

And then they came in dozens—ravens. Hundreds o' ravens. And they settled on the horse's body eatin the body. One by one as they touched the horse's body, every one fell over and died. By this time it was daylight. And Jack could see a castle on the mountains in the distance.

He said, to himself, 'This must be the castle of The Black Thief of Slane.' He wasnae afraid, he made his way there. He wanted to be arrested, he wanted to find the truth for himself. So he travelled on and he came to thes great flagstone steps leadin up to the hill where the castle sat. He was only halfway up when he was immediately arrested by five or six guards and brought in to the great palace of The Black Thief of Slane. He was thrown in a corner and there he lay. And then a door opened. In came this man. He was not a black man. But he was covered in black hair—all his body was covered in black hair, bare from the waist up.

'Aha,' he said, 'another one for my dungeons! Young man, it's your own fault! Nobody told you to come here. But you're goin to my dungeons!'

And Jack stood up. He said, 'Listen, I've been hearin a few, Thief of Slane!'

'Oh,' he said, 'what were you hearin about me, young man?'

He said, 'They tell me you're very strong.'

'Ha ha!' said The Black Thief of Slane. 'Of course I'm strong, I'm the strongest man in all the land in my own territory. I never sent for you, young man! To the peril of your life, you're goin to my dungeons, and by the look of you—you're a well made young man—you'll work hard for me! In my silver mines.'

'Ha,' but Jack said, 'wait a minute! Just a minute, Black Thief, before we start talkin about work.' He said, 'Do you think you're more powerful than me?'

And the Black Thief gied himself a good stretch. He said, 'Of course, my son, would you like to fight?'

Jack says, 'No, I don't want to fight you. Black Thief, I don't want to fight you. But I wouldna mind a bit of a wrastle!'

'A wrastle?'

'Aye,' he said. But Jack said, 'I always wrastle in my bare feet.' Black Thief of Slane had short leather boots on.

'Well,' said the Black Thief, 'if that's what you want, that's what it shall be. But you must eat first!' Oh, The Black Thief of Slane and Jack sat there and they dined together and they had good meat and they talked about many things. And then to this great hall. The Black Thief was stripped to the waist, he never wore anything above his waist. And he took off his boots. He said, 'Well, young man, are you ready?'

Jack said, 'As ready as I'll ever be . . .' Now the old woman had warned Jack, let him throw ye, let him do anything with ye. But make sure that ye get a grip of his toe. So Jack wasna worried, he knew what to do.

So the Black Thief catcht Jack and he threw Jack across the corner, and he threw Jack across his knee. And you know he was just more powerful . . . Jack couldna do very much with him even though Jack was a strong young man. Jack lay on his back and The Black Thief of Slane cam to give him a kick with his foot, and Jack grabbed the big toe. And he hung on with both hands.

The Black Thief screamed in agony! And Jack held and he held and he held. And the Black Thief screamed and he screamed and he screamed. 'Let go,' he said, 'I'll give ye everything I own!' But Jack wouldna let go. And then he got wee-er and wee-er and wee-er and wee-er . . . and Jack held on . . . until there were nothing but a wee drop dust in Jack's hand. The Black Thief was gone.

Jack walked through the palace, nobody stopped him. The guards ran for their life. Here had come the most powerful man, who had slain The Black Thief of Slane! Jack went into the dungeons, set everybody free. Into the mines. They were chained to the wall, old men, young men of all kinds, some naked to the skin, some the flesh hangin off them. And in the middle was a tall young man with blonde golden hair. And Jack walked down. He set them free till he cam to the tall young man, blonde young man.

He said, 'By the way, is your name Ivan?'

And he said, 'Yes, my name is Ivan.'

Jack said, 'I've come to set you free.'

'Oh,' he said, 'at last someone has set me free!'

This was the best lookin young man Jack had ever seen in his life. He had seen princes, he had seen many people in his life, but he never had seen such a good lookin man. He said, 'My friend, you must come with me.' So he turned round to all the people who were slaves, he said, 'The palace is there for ye, the silver mine is there for ye, and everything here! The Black Thief is gone—help yourself to the lot!' And Jack went to the Black Thief's stable and he took two of the best horses he could find. And he gave one to the young blonde Ivan and one to himself. They rode back till they cam to the river. And when they crossed the river, they stopped to give the horses a drink, and there sat an old woman on a stone.

Jack cam up and he dismounted from the horse, and he

said, 'Ivan, just a moment, I have to thank this old woman for what she done for me.'

She said, 'I see ye have returned. And you did what I told ye.'

'Aye,' Jack says, 'thanks to you. If it wasna for you I would never hae managed.'

And she pulled the big old shawl from her head and stood up. There was the most beautifulest young woman you ever saw in all your life! And when she looked at Ivan her eyes lighted up. When Ivan looked at her his eyes lighted up. She says, 'Jack, that Black Thief of Slane was my uncle. And he banned me from his homelands for evermore because I had discovered his terrible secret! And he was afraid that someday I would tell it to someone. So, Jack, I've told it to you.' She said, 'Jack I'll have to come with ye!'

'Oh certainly,' says Jack, 'ye can come with me.'

And Ivan said, 'You can come up on my horse!' So the young woman got up beside Ivan and they rode home. They rode and they rode for many days, and when they came back to the palace the king was overjoyed to see them. He was overjoyed Jack was back and he had rescued the young man. And they wined and dined for many days. As for Ivan, he fell in love with the young woman.

And the king said to Jack, 'Jack, what can I give you?'

'I've no need for anything,' he said, 'my lord.'

And for Ivan and the young woman there was a great wedding. The two of them were married. And Jack stood there to their wedding. And then Ivan took his young woman with him and he set off to find his mother. And they were gone.

Then the king turned to Jack, 'Jack, you've worked hard for me, my son. And,' he said, 'the're something I have to show ye.' So he took Jack up to his bedroom. 'Jack, remember,' he said, and he put his hand under his pillow and he took out the two apples. And he says, 'Jack, look, if ye're ever in trouble, if ye ever feel unwell, remember I'm always here, and the'll be always one for you!' And that's the end of my story.

JACK'S DREAM

I heard this story away in Argyll in the 1930s when I was young. It could have started as a Gaelic story, because Argyll was all Gaelic-speaking at that time. Sunday was a very holy day among the local folk, but to us travelling folk Sunday was just another day. We were religious every day—collecting wir shellfish, poaching wir salmon, guddling wir trout, killing rabbits in the hills, going for sticks, cutting sticks and surviving—according to God who put these things on the land for us. And then in the evenings we just carried on, had wir storytelling sessions just the same. Sunday never changed anything for us. My father's old cousin Willie Williamson told us this Jack tale, a dream story. Traveller men were worse on dreams than traveller women. Sometimes traveller men were ashamed of their dreams because they believed so much in them.

A long time ago in the West Highlands Jack lived in a beautiful little farmhouse. He had everything his heart desired, a beautiful home, all the animals and stock he needed. He had a beautiful young wife. He owned the farm, he owned the land, everything was his own. But the pride of his life was his little son, his baby son. And Jack loved him dearly—he never went to the market, he never went to the fields, he never went anywhere but he took his son along with him. The son was five years old. And of course he loved his daddy, Jack, very much.

97

So after the evening meal, Jack would light his pipe and sit down by the fireside. The thing that Jack loved to do was tell his son stories. Now his baby son, like myself, had grown up with stories, all his life. While Jack's wife was busy doing something else, for she had heard many of his stories—just like yourself—she loved Jack to take her baby son beside him and tell him a story. So one night, here was Jack sitting by the fireside smoking his pipe when his little son comes up.

He says, 'Daddy, tell me a story!'

He said, 'Okay, my little son, I'll tell you a story. Are you sitting comfortable?'

'Okay, Daddy,' he said, 'I'm sitting comfortable.' And he got down on the floor beside his daddy.

'Well,' he said, 'listen to this. You see, my son, you have a wonderful life today, you have everything your heart desires. You have a beautiful home, you have me and your mother, you have everything you need. And someday when I'm gone and your mummy's gone, all this will be yours. We're well-off, we have money, a beautiful farm and all the animals and stock we need. We cannae cope with so many animals we have at the present moment! But son, life was not always like this to me. You see, when I was like your age I was very very poor. And I don't remember my daddy. My daddy died when I was very young. But my poor mother, I remember her well. We had a little tumble-down thatched house,' he said, 'not far from here. And someday I'm going to take you and show ye the room where I was born. The walls is still there and the house 's still mine. Someday I'll take ye and show ye it, where your granny and I lived a long time ago. So I'm going to tell you why we are so well off today. You see, my poor mother she worked and strived very hard to bring me up. She sent me to school and she did everything within her power she could for me. And she was a wonderful mother to me. But we were never very rich. We never had much money to spend. Of course I didna worry about money in these days,

I didna know what money was. Because my mother supplied everything for me.

'But then one night,' he said, 'as I lay on my little bed of straw, which was just a straw mattress, I had a wonderful dream. Now by this time I was seventeen years old.' And Jack's little baby son's cuddling up beside his daddy. Jack chapped his pipe on the fire, on the hearth of stone and he filled it again. He had a wonderful dream. 'And,' he said, 'I wakened up in the morning. That dream was so pure to me. I could see it, but I never told my mother about it. Because my mother was a great one for dreams. And she would want to find faults with my dreams. So the next night, my son, I went to bed again, and there I had the same dream all over again!' The little son's listening. 'And then the next night I went to bed again I dreamt the same thing again! Three nights! Now, my son,' he said, 'if you dream something three nights in a row, the're bound to be something in your dream!

'So next morning I was sitting at my breakfast with my mummy—a little bit of porridge and an egg—and she said, "Jack, what's troubling you this morning, my little son?"

"Well, Mother, I had a terrible dream."

She says, "Son, tell me your dream."

"Ach, Mother," I said, "you'll no probably be interested in my dream."

"Of course, my son," she said, "I'll be interested in your dream, because dreams are very important. Sometimes they can come true!"

"But all the dreams I've ever had, Mother, have never come true."

She says, "Tell me anyway."

"Well," I said, "Mother, for three nights I've lain in my bed and I've dreamed . . . of a little village and a graveyard and a little church . . . every night my steps take me to that little graveyard and that little church. And there in my dream I was supposed to find my fortune."

'Oh,' his mother said, 'queer. How many times did you dream this?'

'Mother,' Jack said, 'it was so plain. A little village, little thatch houses and a little churchyard and a little church and a lot of stones standing, tombstones in the graveyard. And there everything keeps telling me, if I go to the churchyard I will find my fortune.'

She said, 'Son, that's queer. It's only a dream!'

'Well,' he said, 'Mother, it may only be a dream to you. But I cannae rest with the three nights dreaming this dream. I have to go . . . But, Mother, I've never been in that village.'

She says, 'Explain it to me.'

'Well,' he says, 'there's a river and a bridge. There's a bend in the road. And you go up a little brae and the're a little village. There's a farm and there's a few thatched cottages. Down below the cottages is a little church.'

'Oh son!' she says. 'That's the church where me and your father got married!'

'Mother,' he said, 'is it far fae here?'

'Ah,' she says, 'laddie, about, I would say at least twenty miles fae here. And you've never been in it.'

'Well,' he says, 'Mother, I'm going! I must go to that church, Mother, for the sake o' my own mind, for the sake o' my ain thoughts, I've got to go to this church. And I'm going to stay there, Mother, till I find my fortune.'

'But laddie,' she said, 'where are you going to find your fortune in a graveyard?'

'Well, Mother,' he says, 'I cannae help it. I cannae have peace of mind . . .' So anyway, as there werena much tae dae around the wee place where Jack and his mother stayed, the next morning she made him a wee parcel of meat to take with him, some bannock and a wee bit o' bacon or an egg or two.

'Okay, laddie,' she says, 'but take care o' yourself. Remember . . . not that much'll come ower you where you're gaun to—it's only a wee village and it's mostly people in the village are only shepherds and crofters. They'll no do you any harm. And to tell you the God's truth, I dinnae ken a single soul in the village. I cannae remember naebody but the auld sexton that used to take care of the churchyard, that's the only one I remember. Ach, he'll probably be deid by this time, Jack. He was an old man a long time ago when me and your father was married.' But Jack couldna rest. He would make his way. His mother gied him the directions, and he set sail.

'Ach,' he said, 'Mother, I'll find shelter. Give me enough meat tae keep me gaun for three days. I'll stay three days and I'll come back. If naething happens, my mind'll be completely clear.' So he said good-bye to his mother. His mother had parcelled him a wee puckle meat. Now Jack was sitting telling his wee laddie this story. 'This is your granny I'm talking about,' he said. The wee laddie's sitting listening, see!

So Jack kissed his mother good-bye and off he went. And he travelled on. Jack was a good walker. He was a young handsome man, only seventeen years old. He travelled on, he travelled on and that night he slept in an old barn. The next day he travelled on, a beautiful sunny day. And sure as God, by the next morning he landed in the little village. He came over the little bridge, there was the little burn in his dream, he'd never been there before in his life. And up the little brae, there was the little farm and there was the thatched houses. He looked down, on the left hand side and there he could see the steeple of a wee church. 'This is the place in my dream,' says Jack.

So Jack walked down to the little churchyard. There was a little dyke round it, a dry-stone dyke. And he leaned over the dyke, looked into the old churchyard. There was a wee church in the yard, and he stood there and felt so peaceful thinking to himself—what kind of people were buried there a long time ago? There were old stones, some with names

101

that were readable and some with names that the weather had worn away. But the little church was still there. Jack looked in away at the side—he saw an old man with a scythe with a grey beard down to there—he was cutting the grass with a scythe. But the old man never spoke.

So Jack stayed all day, and he had a wee bit tart left his mother gien him, a wee bit meat. And that night he slept in the barn on the farm. The next day he spent all his day again leaning over the dyke of the yard. Sometimes he'd lean over this part of the dyke, sometimes he'd wander round and lean ower the other part. But two days passed and Jack begint to think to himself, 'There's nothing here but a graveyard. My mother was right. There's nothing in my dream that's true. But it's still in my mind.'

But anyway, back to the same barn again, and he slept in the barn that night. He finished his last bit o' meat his mother gien him. Because it was summertime, the nights were very short, Jack thought he should go back to the graveyard again for the third day. And this is what he did. Back he went to the graveyard, he leaned over the dyke for an hour staring at the graves, deep in thought thinking about the people that was buried there, people he would loved to have met. He wandered round and leaned over this part, and he still watched the old man cutting away with his scythe. Then the sun begint to rise in the sky. And the old man picked up his scythe, and he looked up at Jack, into his eyes for the first time in three days. He came walking over to Jack.

He says, 'Young man, excuse me! But I've been watching you. You see, I've been watching you for the last three days.'

And Jack said, 'I've been watching you! You're good with the scythe. I'm a bit of a scytheman myself.'

'Oh well,' he says, 'I have to keep the grass down in the churchyard.' And Jack could see he was very old, well up in his seventies or eighties. He says, 'Young man, I know you've got a trouble. I can see worry in your face. I know you've got a problem.' And the old man took his scythe and leaned it against the dyke. He sat down and put his back against the dyke. He said, 'Young man, sit down! And tell me, what's your problem. I've been watching you for three long days. You've been leaning over that dyke. Hae ye somebody buried in here belonging to ye?'

Jack says, 'No. There's naebody buried in here belonging to me. But my mother was married in this church a long time ago.'

'Oh,' he said, 'she was, oh aye. Well then, my laddie, there's been many people married in this church, as long as my time. I've been working in this churchyard for fifty years.'

Jack says, 'It's a lang lang time.'

'It is a lang time, laddie, but,' he says, 'someday I'll end up here tae amang my auld freends. But come, tell me, why have ye spent three long days leaning ower the church dyke in three parts o' the wall looking at the church if ye naebody buried in here?'

'Well,' Jack said, 'I'm kind o' shamet to admit it. But do you believe in dreams, old man?'

'Well, depends on the dream,' he says. 'Was it a dream that brought you here?'

Jack said, 'Aye, it was a dream that brought me here. Ye see, old man, three nights I dreamed the same dream. I saw your church, I saw your graveyard, I saw your village in my dream. And I've never been here in my life. And in my dream I was supposed to find my fortune at this churchyard.'

'Oh laddie,' he says, 'the're no much a fortune round here for ye. The're no much here. But onyway, never mind about dreams, laddie! Dreams is dreams. But I'll tell ye—I had a dream myself! And a queerer dream a body could never have! Just when you brought it up . . . a long time ago. And for three nights that dream cam back to me, laddie, and I got a bit worried about it tae. But I worried about it for a long time, but finally I got it oot o' my mind.'

'Well,' Jack says tae him, 'now I've tellt you my dream, would you tell me yours?'

'Ach well, laddie,' he says, 'I suppose there's nae harm in telling my dream. I just treat it as nonsense.'

Jack said, 'How long ago since you've dreamed this dream?'

'Ah,' he says, 'laddie, laddie, a long time ago I dreamed this dream. I must hae been about, I would be a wee bit older 'an you when I dreamed it, but I still think about it sometimes. It's still in my memory.'

Jack said, 'Would you like to tell me about it?'

'Ach well,' he said, 'seeing as there's no much . . . we're sitting here and I'll soon be finished onyway, and there's nae harm . . . treating it as innocent dreams.' He said, 'My dream was a dream that was awfae strange. You see, I dreamt I was passing a wee thatched cottage and I stopped there and I asked for a drink of water. An old woman cam oot o' the cottage with a sheet apron on her, grey hair and she gied me a drink oot o' a clay jug. And I passed on. Then I cam in my dream tae a tree. Noo,' he said, 'laddie, this is the funniest tree I ever seen in my life. Because this tree wasnae just a common tree. This tree at one time had been a young sapling, when somebody took it and tied it in a knot. It was a complete knot as if you were tying a knot in a bit string! And in my dream I seen that tree as plain as could be. Beside the tree was standing a shovel, a rusty old shovel. And that was my dream. Now,' he said, 'I'd never been there before. I dinnae ken where the place is. But I seen that tree, laddie, as plain as I'm seeing you . . . Well, laddie, I think it's time I was awa then, because my old wife'll be waiting. But it's been good cracking to you. And I hope,' he said, 'you'll mak your fortune someday!'

And Jack's heart begint to beat with excitement. His heart begint to pat as fast as could be. Because Jack knew in his heart he had seen that tree himself. So he bade the old man good-bye and shaked hands with him. (And Jack's wee son's sitting by his side listening to every word!) So Jack said good-bye to the old sexton in the churchyard and he said, 'I made my way hame to my mother. And your granny was very happy to see me back. She asked me a lot of questions and I tellt her about the old man, I tellt her about the crack in the graveyard. But I never mentioned the tree.'

But he says, 'Ye'll no believe this, son, but tomorrow morning I'm going to tak ye and I'm going to show you that tree. And you've never seen a tree like this before in all your life. Because I promised you someday that I would take ye and show ye my mother's old hoose where I was born. And tomorrow I'm going to show you the tree!

'So with the excitement when the old man tellt me his dream, because that tree was only about twenty yards from my mother's old hoose, I had hurried back and never tellt my mother about the tree. I told her about the church, I told her about the village. And she asked me how many people I'd met. I said I only met the old sexton at the church. And I never told my mother about the sexton's dream, because I knew where the tree was!

'So after a wee bite with my mother, I said, "Mother, I have to go for a wee walk to myself." So I walked up, and you'll no believe this, laddie, I had seen that tree many, many times, but I paid no attention tae it. But I always looked at it because when it was a sapling it was a wee rowan tree, and when it was only a young sapling somebody had took it and tied it in a knot and left it. The years had passed by, probably long afore I was born, the tree grew thick and strong—but it was still tied in a knot—the most beautiful knot you ever saw in all your life, laddie! I couldna wait to go up to that old tree. And when I walked up to it, what do you think I seen? A wee bit o' rusty iron sticking out from the root of the tree. And I scraped away the earth with my hands, and there was the head of an old spade! But the handle was gone. For years had passed, the wood had worn away. But the metal was left—it was rusty—the head of the spade was there.

'So just for curiosity sake I took the spade, the head of it and I begint to dig round the tree. And you'll no believe this, laddie,' he said, 'the spade hit something. And I looked. I pulled back the earth with my hand. There under the earth beside the tree with the knot was an iron box! With the excitement beating in my heart I pulled up the box. It was old and it was rusty. And when I opened it, laddie, it was full of gold sovereigns, hundreds of them! And I carried it back to my mother. Me and your granny sat and we cleaned every one up. We had as much money that we'll ever need i' all wir life. Then I took that old shovel and I covered back the earth I'd took from under that tree.

'So I moved in and bought this farm for all that money. And I gave your old granny the best life she ever had in all her life till she finally died. And I gave her a lovely funeral. That's where all the money cam from that I have today. Some day it will all be yours. And tomorrow morning you and me will pack a wee bit o' sandwich with us or a wee bit of lunch from your mother. We'll go for a walk and I'll take ye to that tree, the tree that was not in my dream, but in an old sexton's dream—that took me from the churchyard to my own home.' And that's the story Jack told to his baby son.

JACK AND THE POTTER'S GIFT

Now in the many wonderful Jack tales you'll find Jack can talk to the king, Jack can talk to the princess, Jack can go afore the court of law in stories that are to follow later. But this story begins a little time before these stories, where Jack became known as a great talker. Now talking is the very thing that people today are interested in, how people can express themselves, how they think. And I hope by listening to this story you might learn something. When you go to your school class, when you go to your room, when you talk with your friends, always think about what like poor Jack was when he went to his first school, when he went to visit his friends. Because Jack in my story was uncouth. His talk was rough and uneducated. He didn't mind what he was saying. So this is what happened.

You see, a long time ago away by a little village in the country Jack lived with his old mother. Oh, they had a little croft together, they kept a few cows and a few sheep. Oh, Jack was very happy with his mother. He 'tended the local school. But the teacher and the school master were always finding complaints, because as far as they were concerned Jack was the worst talker in all the world. Jack never seemed to say things right!

Jack and his mother were well to do. His old daddy had died and left a little money, a few stock and a croft, a little bit of land. But the little house where Jack lived was down in a valley. To reach the village you had to climb a brae, a little hill, it seemed to go up into the mountains. And people had always called it 'Potter's Brae'. Now Jack had to walk up that brae because the school was in the village up on the top of the hill. From the little croft down in the hollow of the valley, a twisting steep brae went up. On the top of the hill was a small store and a school Jack had attended. But as my story tells you Jack had climbed that brae many, many times.

Every time he sat down with his mummy to have his meal in the house at night-time he would always ask, 'Mother, why do they call it Potter's Brae?'

'Well,' she said, 'laddie, that I couldna tell you. Look, as far as I'm concerned I havena a clue why they call it Potter's Brae.'

Now Jack had left school, he was busy looking after the croft for his mother. And every Monday morning the first thing he would do was to take a little bag and walk up that brae to go to the village to get groceries for his mother, what they needed for the week, maybe a bit tobacco for his mother's pipe, a few messages, a bit o' cheese and butter and things like that. He would bring a basket o' eggs to the village store and trade them for a little money. And things with Jack and his mother were going on fine. No problem. Till one morning.

It was the very first day of April! And of course the first day of April is an old tradition, goes back a long way in Scotland—April's Fool. You know about the April's Fool. In Scottish words they call it 'Gowk's Day'.

So after breakfast Jack's mother said, 'Laddie, I need ye tae gang tae the village today.' And she gied him some money, ye see. She gied him a half gold sovereign. 'Now,' she said, 'laddie, dinnae loss it.' Because Jack was a kind of 'come-hither' kind o' lad, ye know! Come hither—he didna give a damn what happened! So he took the gold sovereign. She said, 'Look, check your pockets now, laddie, see the're nae holes in your pockets!'

'Mother,' he said, 'you sewed my pockets five or six times this week already,' because Jack was always losin things in his pockets. And his mother seen this, the one thing she always took care o', she sewed Jack's pockets. Because if she ever gied him a coin, he sure was to lose it.

'Now,' she warned him, 'look, Jack, when ye gang to the village, would you be a wee bit polite to the folk?'

'Mother,' he says, 'What fir? What am I gaunna be polite fir? They're just folk like me and you.' Jack was a wee bit uncouth with his speech. And this had troubled many people, his school master, his school teacher and the people of the village. And some people laughed behind their hands at Jack, you know, the way he spoke.

They said, 'He'll never grow up to be a doctor, he'll never grow up to be a lawyer, he'll never grow up to be nothing! He'll be a crofter all his life, because he hasna got the speech fine enough for anyone.' In bygone days, you don't know, to be a good talker in ancient Scotland was a wonderful thing—to have the 'gift of the gab' was a wonderful thing! You could never be a minister unless you could talk. You could never be a lawyer unless you could talk. You could never be a doctor unless you could talk. And Jack's mother had never set nae plans for Jack because she knew it didna matter what she said to Jack . . . Some of the things that Jack said to his mother when she sent him for messages wouldna be very polite, you know! He had a wee bit swear word for everything he said, you know. These old four-letter words when he mentioned everything, you know!

So after Jack gets his breakfast in the morning she says, 'Laddie, now remember, I want tobacco for my pipe!'

'Of course you want yir bloody tobacco, Mother,' he says. 'Div I ever forget yir bloody tobacco?' It was bloody this and bloody that, *f*'in this and *f*'in that.

She says, 'Laddie, your language is going to get you into trouble some day.'

109

'Ach, Mother,' he says, 'wha's f'in carin' aboot language! Naebody f'in worries what happens!' You know, this is the way Jack carried on!

Anyway, she said, 'Remember now my tobacco. I'm no caring what you get else.'

But he said, 'I'll get all you f'in need!' You know! Because that's the way he was brought up. So anyway, he takes the half sovereign from his mother, puts it in his pocket, gets a wee bag fae his mother and he starts up Potter's Brae.

Now Potter's Brae was a long brae. Ye had to climb the brae and then ye cam to a bend. When you climbed there was a hill going straight up and then there was a bad bend, then straight up was another bend, and then up to the wee village on the top of the hill. With the half-sovereign in his pocket he called back cheerio to his mother. 'I'll no be long, Mother,' he said, 'I'll no be f'in long.' He always used the swear words when he spoke to his mother. And off he went.

So time travelled on. He climbed the first bend. But when he came to the second corner to turn into the second bend, lo and behold—Jack looked in amazement. For sitting by the roadside was a wee man. It was the strangest little man Jack had ever seen in all his life. He had never seen a man dressed like this. Now to explain. Beside the little man was a large wooden wheelbarrow, like the barrow farmers would use a long time ago for their dung or hurling neeps. It was a solid wooden wheel cut from a log. The sides of the wooden barrow were deep. And there sitting by the barrow was the strangest little man Jack had ever seen. He had little thin legs with these skin-tight trousers to below his knee. But his shoes were larger than any Jack had ever seen, with big shiny buckles. He had a little jerkin on his shoulder and it was all full of these kind of strips and straps—like you see on the man on a pack of cards, the jester—he was dressed like a joker. He had a long narrow face, bright blue eyes and long golden hair down his back. And he's sitting

110

cross-legged beside this empty wheelbarrow, a barrow larger than himself.

When Jack drew level with him climbing the brae, he said, 'Good morning, Jack!'

Jack stopped. And Jack looked and gazed at the little man that was dressed like the jester, the funniest and strangest dressed little man Jack had ever seen in his life. He said, 'Excuse me, mister, but do you ken me?'

And the little man who was very polite said, 'Of course, young man, I know all about you. You're Jack from the village. I've heard about you and they tell me you walk this way many times.'

Jack was amazed at the way the little man talked. He had never heard anyone talk so politely in all his life. Because I told you Jack was very uncouth. If the man had said, 'I climb this bloody hill every day in the week,' it would have been down on Jack's terms. But this was not the talk Jack had heard before. He was the most polite little man Jack had ever seen. 'Well,' he said, 'wee mannie, wha' do you want fae me? I'm on ma way to the village.'

'Oh I know, Jack,' he said, 'you're on your way to the village. It wouldn't be troubling too much, my little friend, would you give me a little help?'

Jack says, 'What kind o' help would you seek of me, wee mannie?'

He said, 'Jack, I'm wondering if you would hurl my barrow to the top of the brae?'

'Hurl your barra, wee mannie?' he said. 'Of course I'll hurl your barra fir ye! Nae problem avaa, man!' Jack spoke a very rough talk. 'The're nae bother avaa, man, tae hurl your wee barra tae the top o' the brae. It'll be a pleasure tae me, man, it'll keep me walkin onyway!'

'All right,' says the wee man.

And Jack got a haud o' the handles o' the barrow and the wee man jumped up on the shaft. And Jack said, 'Are ye wantin a wee hurl, wee mannie, are ye tired? It's nae

111

problem avaa.' So Jack got the two handles o' the barrow and he hurled it up. Of course the road up the hill was very rough. There were bumps and rocks and holes in the road, because in these bygone days the roads were very rough. And the wheel was going into bumps. It was a solid block of wood for the wheel. This barrow was very old. And as far as the wee man looked he was very old. But Jack never paid much attention to this. Anyway, the barrow went up into a hole in a bump in the road.

And the wee man said, 'Stop, stop, Jack, stop! Jack, stop, please I beg of you!'

So Jack stopped. 'Eh, what's wrong with you, mannie?' he said.

He said, 'They're all falling out! You've lost them. Half of them's lying on the roadway!'

And Jack looked around. He couldna see a thing. Jack said, 'Wee mannie, there's naething lyin on the road. Look, the barra was empty when I hurled you up the brae. The're nothing in't!'

He says, 'Jack you don't know who I am!'

Jack said, 'No, I've never seen the like of you in all my life.'

He said, 'I'm Mister Potter! And this is my hill—called after me—this is Potter's Brae. And I've been out all morning far down the valley collecting all the words, and packed them in my barrow. Now you careless uncouth youth—you've spilled them all!'

'Spilled them all?' says Jack. 'Spilled what? There's nothing there, mannie. Yir barra's empy!'

'Oh Jack,' he said, 'I see. You do not understand. Just stop a moment.' And the wee man sat on the handles o' the barrow. He says, 'Jack, sit down here beside me! I want to talk to you.'

But Jack said, 'I've got to get to the village for my mother's messages.'

'Oh,' says the wee mannie, 'dinnae worry! You'll have

plenty time to get for your mother's messages. You take me to the top of the hill after we have a little talk, and I'll give you a wonderful gift.'

'A gift?' says Jack thinking to himself. 'Maybe money. Maybe he'll give me money. Maybe he'll mak me rich. I'll never need tae worry again anymore.'

So Jack sat down by the side of the barrow, and the wee man said, 'Listen, Jack, very carefully. I want to talk to you. You see, Jack, a long time ago when first I came to this place there were not many people. And there was not a school room in this place. There were not a village in this place. *There were nothing in this place, Jack, only me. And I was young, just like you. And I was careless just like you. And I didn't care, just like you, Jack. I didn't care nothing. But you see, then I wanted to learn things, Jack. I wanted to know what people said to each other. So I listened and I learned.* And now I am the collector of all the missing words, the missing letters, of course, Jack.'

'Missing letters, wee man,' he says, 'what do you mean?'

'Well you see, Jack,' said the wee man, 'as you know my name is Mister Potter, and this is my brae. Sometimes people who likes to talk likes to drop all those words when they speak. They like to drop letters, they don't talk correctly! And this is a hard job for me when people don't talk correctly. Because then they drop a word, maybe some people has a lisp in their speech. And then they drop a letter. I've got all the trouble to pick that letter up, put it in my barrow, hurl it to the top of my hill. And then save them all up, and give them back to the people so that the next time they can pronounce their words purely.'

'Oh,' Jack said, 'mister, mister, you must have a hard problem!'

'Well,' he says, 'Jack, it's no such a hard problem as you think it is. But that's my job. But please, help me!'

Jack said, 'What can I help—there's nothing I can see?'

'Well,' he said, 'I know, Jack, you can't see them. But

113

I'll collect them. But be very careful!' So the wee man got down on his knees and he's going along the road, picking these things up and he's putting them in the barrow. And he's lifting them all up and putting them in the barrow—*h*s and *p*s and *q*s and *t*s and *m*s and *l*s—and he's packing them. He's lifting them, mentioning them, as he's picking them up and putting them in the barrow. 'Now be very careful,' he says, 'Jack, it won't hold another one!'

Jack looked at the barrow. The barrow was empty.

Anyhow, 'Now,' he says, 'Jack, that's them all gotten at last!' So once again the wee man Mr Potter climbed up on the shafts of the barrow. And he said, 'Jack, on your way! But please be very careful!'

So Jack avoided all the holes and all the ruts and he guided that barrow to the top of the hill till he came to the first of the village.

'Stop!' said this little man. 'This is as far as we go! You have done well, Jack,' he said. 'You've been very very careful.'

'Well,' Jack said, 'thanks for that.'

'Now Jack,' he said, 'I have to leave you. But Jack, before I leave you I'm going to give you a gift. *A wonderful gift, that will stand you all your life. From this moment on you will have my gift.* And now I must leave you.' Then the wee man took the barrow and he hurled it over the side of the road. And Jack looked . . . he was gone.

Jack scratched his head and he said, 'God, what a terrible exper— . . . what a terrible experience I've had. What's this—what am I saying? What am I saying? What a terrible experience I've had! Oh dear,' he says, 'this is terrible! Where has he gone? What happened to him?'

But he walked on to the little store. And when he got into the store all these old women from the village were there. All the old men were in buying their things. And in walks Jack with his mother's bag. When they saw Jack coming into the store they all stepped aside. Because when Jack used to walk to the store he would say, 'Get oot o' my *f*'in way.' You

114

know, he pushed all the people aside him. So Jack stood in the shop behind everybody with his bag in his hand. 'Excuse me, madam,' he said, 'eh, after you!'

The people stared in amazement. This was Jack. And then a man came in, 'I'm needing a wee bit tobacco for my pipie, missus,' he said.

Jack said, 'After you, sir! Please, go ahead!'

And everybody stared in amazement. They wondered—this was magic! What happened to Jack? What had happened to him? So after everybody was served he stood.

He said, 'Eh, my dear, my madam, I am sorry, but I need a little few things for my mother, please. And I wonder, she would like some tobacco and such and such, and such and such. And thank you very much. And I'm sure if you don't mind, I have plenty time to spare . . .' Jack talked like a lawyer!

The word soon spread along the village after Jack had got all his messages. He thanked the lady very much, walked back to his mother with his bit o' messages. But that was not the end of the story. Jack was never again to come into contact with Mr Potter. But Jack was to become one of the finest speakers in all the country! When a gathering got together and somebody wanted someone to give a speech, who did they call on but Jack! Because Jack had gotten a gift. Jack had told no one. But Jack never again mentioned to his mother who was Mister Potter, and why was it called Potter's Brae!

JACK AND THE THREE DRUNKEN ELVES

Travellers respected a man who drank. They didna want their sons to be alcoholics. But you couldna sit at a campfire and have a story or a tale without having a drink. When a traveller told a tale about Jack drinking, they always said, 'The mother was down upon him for drinking,' and she was always against it. They were referring to their own mother or their son's mother. But in the stories when Jack coaxed his mother to drink with him, she would—just to keep him with her! Because traveller women hated to lose their sons. Even to this present day, mothers like to keep their sons. Let him be a drunkard, let him be anything under the sun. It's the thought that he's a part of things that really fit in life, and without him things seem to fall apart.

Jack lived with his mother in a little house in the corner of the forest. And Jack, like me, was a drunkard. Every penny Jack could find, he would spend it on drink. He coaxed his mother, event his mother's pension. When he used to go and lift his mother's pensions a' the week-end, he would try and get a pint of beer or a bottle of something off it.

And she says tae him, 'Jack, ye know son, you're ruinin yir life by drinkin.'

'Oh, Mother,' he said, 'dinnae tell me these things. Mither, look,' he said tae her, 'I dinnae remember my faither.'

'No, son, I know ye dinnae remember yir faither,' she

said. 'He too was fond o' a wee drink. But it was the cause
o' his daith.'

But he said, 'If it was the cause o' my faither's death, what
difference does it mak tae me? I dinnae mind on my faither.
What did my faither dae?'

'Look,' she said, 'Jack, sit down there beside me, son. I
ken ye like a wee drink.'

He said tae her, 'Mither, dinnae think about me haein a
drink . . . when had you got a drink last?'

She says, 'Laddie, I never had a drink since yir faither
dee'd.'

He says, 'How long ago was that?'

She says, 'Seven year ago.'

'Well, Mither,' he said, 'I'm gaun to the toon the nicht. And
I'm gaunnae make sure that you're gaunna get drunk when I
come back from the toon! Ye any money about ye, Mither?
Hae ye got coppers in yir pocket o' ony description?'

She said, 'I got my pension today—five shillings.'

But he says, 'Ye sellt some eggs, Mother.'

'Aye, I've seven shillings,' she said.

He says, 'Mither, gie me the seven shillings. I'll gie it back,
I'll gie ye it back again. God, I'm dyin for a . . . I'm goin to
the toon and I'm dyin for a wee drink.'

She said, 'Curse upon ye, Jack.' But she loved Jack, ye
ken, it was her baby. She loved him, would give him anything
in her heart. 'On ye go,' she said, 'the're the seven shillings
tae ye! Tak it wi ye and dae what ye like wi it.'

Away goes Jack tae the toon. Seven shillings in these days
was an awfa lot o' money. And Jack goes to the pub and he has
a drink and a sing-song and a carry-oot. But he never forgets
his old mother! And he buys a half-bottle o' whisky, which
cost him a shilling and a sixpence. He goes back, wanderin
up the road and a half-bottle in his pocket.

Noo, by the time he wandert back to his wee mother's croft
he begint to get kind o' sober, ye see? The drink that he had
got in the pub was begint to wear off him. And he says tae

117

hissel, 'Will I tak a wee taste of my mother's wee drop, or will I no tak it? Na,' he said, 'I couldna touch her wee drop o' whisky, I'd better bring it back tae her.' Now three times he put his hand doon to tak his mother's wee nip, and three times he put his hand back again. 'Na, na,' he said, 'I couldna dae it, I couldna dae it!' But anyway, he lands hame, hame tae his mother's hoose.

His mother was sitting, the table was set. She had a wee drop o' meat fir him and a wee taste o' supper. But Jack wasna very interested in the supper. He was interested in the half-bottle he had in his pocket.

She says, 'Aye, Jack, ye're back.'

'Aye, Mother,' he said, 'I'm back.'

She said, 'Did ye have a good time?'

'Aye, Mother,' he said, 'I had a good time tae masel. I definitely had a good time tonight. I met a lot of folk in the pub and I had a good drink. And I've brung ye back a wee half-bottle o' whisky. Gie me a wee cup!' She gied him a wee cup and he gied her a wee drink. And he had a wee drink hissel.

She said, 'Are ye wantin any supper?'

He said, 'I'm no wantin any supper, Mother, nae supper o' nae kind.'

She says, 'Well, Jack, what do ye really want?'

'I dinnae want nothing, Mother,' he said. 'I only want you to enjoy yourself.' So the two o' them sat and cracked. He said, 'Mother, tell me a wee story, tell me something about my faither.'

'Well,' she said, 'Jack, I'll tell ye a wee bit about yir faither. Look, yir faither was a good man, and me and him had a good goin croft here. We were workin it properly. And one day yir father went oot to the moor. He never touched drink fir months, fir months never touched a drink! And one night he cam back fae the moor, he was blind miraculous drunk. Miraculous drunk! He had a wee barrel on his back, and he had it below his oxter. He put it up on the mantelpiece there.

And,' she said, 'I never paid much attention to it. I didna think . . . I thought it was a wee ornament or something he'd brung back. But every time I went up to it, it was empty. I didna see nae harm intae it. But every day fae then on, yir faither was drunk fir evermore. And fae that day on, yir faither drank hissel to the grave. And that's why, Jack, that I dinnae like you drinkin noo.'

'But,' he says, 'Mother, what happened to the barrel?'

'Jack,' she says, 'that's one thing I cannae tell ye. Efter yir faither dee'd, the barrel disappeared. And I never seen it fir evermore.'

He says, 'Mither, what kind o' barrel was it? Was it big?'

'No,' she says, 'it wasna big, it was only a wee barrel that size. And it set on the mantelpiece there, and every time I went to it, it was empty. But every time yir faither went to it, it was full. It must hae been full, because every time I cam in, he was drunk!'

'But,' he says, 'Mother, will you tell me something? Whaur did my father get it?'

She says, 'Jack, son, I couldna tell ye. But he must hae got it oot on the moor some place.'

So the next morning there werena much tae do about the wee croft and Jack went away for a walk on the moor. And he's thinkin about this, ye see? He's thinkin about his barrel. He couldna get it oot o' his mind. And he was fond o' a drink, oh, Jack was fond o' his drink! He walked away for miles into the moor. And he cam to this bonnie wee patch among the heather. It was clear among the heather, and he sat doon. The sun was shinin frae the heavens, ye see! He lay back with his hand below his heid. And he was thinkin about his life, he was thinkin about what his mother tellt him and his father's wee barrel, and thinkin about everything. Lo and behold, brother, he fell sound asleep, sound asleep.

He must hae slept for a long, long time, but he wakened. He sat up. Something disturbed him. And when he sat up he

119

looked round him. Here was three wee men, three wee toy men that size! About six inches tall. And one was sittin on this shouder, and one was sittin on that shouder, and one was sittin on his chest. He rubbed his heid in amazement. Because he was amazed! For Jack had never seen three wee men like this before. And he was all excited. The three wee men spoke tae him.

'Dinnae worry, Jack,' they said, 'dinnae worry, son, dinnae worry!'

He said, 'Wha are youse?'

'Oh Jack,' he said, 'dinnae bother, dinnae worry yourself! Dinnae be excited. Would you like a drink?'

'Ha hah!' said Jack. 'Would I like a drink? Whaur am I gaunnae get a drink? Whaur am I gaunnae get a drink in this world? And whaur in the name of God, am I asleep or am I drunk or am I stupid, whaur did youse come fae?'

'Never mind, Jack,' he said, 'about . . . one thing at a time. Take a wee drink first and we'll talk about it afterwards.'

So the three wee men cam up and they held a wee barrel that size. 'Jist take a wee drink, Jack!' And he held the wee barrel. Jack took the wee barrel to his mooth and he whoooooooogh, and he feelt the heat gaun down his chest, he feelt the heat gaun down. He feelt this amazin feelin spreadin ower his body. And he begint to be a wee bit peevie, you see! And the three wee men's still sittin. He said, 'Was that good?'

'Brother dear,' says Jack, 'was that good? Ye any mair?'

'No,' says the three wee men, 'Jack, ye're no gettin nae mair. Brother, you cannae get nae mair!'

Jack said, 'In the name of God, what was in that barrel ye gied me?'

'Jack,' he said, 'we gied ye some Elfin Whisky.'

Jack said, 'Look, hae ye got ony mair Elfin Whisky ye could gie me? Could ye gie me one more sup?'

'No,' says the three wee men, 'ye're not gettin one more sup the night! I'll tell ye what we'll dae wi you,' he said. 'We'll gie ye another sup if ye mak a promise tae us.'

Jack said, 'Fir a taste o' that stuff, I'd promise my soul tae the devil!'

'Well,' he said, 'Jack, ye can have a drink wonst more out o' the barrel if ye give us one promise—will you come wi hus?'

Says Jack, 'Gie me another sook oot o' the barrel and I'll go wi you anywhere under the sun!'

So the three wee men held up this barrel to Jack, and Jack took another drink, glug-glug, glug-glug. And the wee man catcht it and took it back from Jack. 'Now dinnae drink too much, Jack!' he said. And Jack feelt the wonderful glow, and it gaed doon through his body, it spread through his heid and he feelt he was floatin on air. And these three wee men's still sittin.

'Now, boys,' Jack said, 'what is it?' See, noo he was in good order!

'Well, Jack,' he said, 'I'll tell ye the truth. Look, we're elves.'

'Well,' said Jack, 'ye're bound to be something, because I've never seen youse before, I dinnae ken what youse are.'

'Well, Jack,' he said, 'we're elves. And many many years ago your faither did a good turn fir us. But we'll no talk about that. But, Jack, wad ye come wi us and dae one turn fir us? And look, we'll give you anything you want.'

Jack said, 'I dinnae ken what ye can gie me, but wad ye gie me another wee sook o' the barrel? And I'll dae anything under the sun!'

'No,' say the elves, 'ye're no gettin another taste o' the barrel. Nothing!'

Jack said, 'Look, gie me one sup, and I'll go with ye tae the end of the earth!'

'No,' says the three wee men, 'ye're no gettin another taste!'

'Well,' Jack said, 'what is it ye want me tae dae? I'll dae anything under the sun fir ye, I'll gie ma soul fir youse!' he said. An' they were only that size.

'Jack,' he says, 'look, listen tae this what I'm gaun to tell ye. We come fae Elfland and we're three elves. And we're three guards. We were guardin the king's treasure, and we always spent wir entire life guardin it. And one night us three got drunk and the king's treasure went a-missin. It was gone for ever! And the king banned us from Elfland, we can never go back anymore. But he said one thing and made us one promise—if we can bring a mortal, human being back tae Elfland, that can tell us what happened tae the treasure . . . because only a mortal is gaunnae ken what happened— then, he said, we'll be back and installed in the king's good favour for ever after. Noo, Jack,' he said, 'would you come back wi us tae Elfland? Would ye come back wi hus and try and discover what happened tae the king's treasure?'

Noo Jack hadna got a clue! He hadna got one clue what happened to the king's treasure. 'Well,' he said, 'it's a task ye're giein me. But look, I'm willin. My mother'll prob'ly be asleep by this time and she'll no ken whaur I am. But, would ye gie me one sip o' the barrel before I go?'

'Okay,' say the elves, 'on one condition, if ye come back wi hus.'

So the three elves held the barrel and Jack took another sip of the Elfin Whisky. He feelt this heat comin doon through his body and he's floatin on air! He said, 'Lead on! Lead on!'

So the three wee elves say, 'Okay, I'll tell ye what,' they said tae him. 'Jack, two o' us'll go in front o' ye and one'll go behind ye, so's you cannae make a mistake.' They wouldna trust him, ye see. 'Two o' hus'll go in front, and one behind ye and we'll lead ye to Elfland.'

'Fair enough!' says Jack.

But he says, 'Look, Jack, there's one thing ye must under- stand. You cannae come back to Elfland as big as that! Ye'll never get there. You'll have to wait a wee minute . . .' And this wee man had a scalloped belt round his middle, a belt with fringes on it. And aside o' his belt he had a wee toy bottle. He took oot the wee bottle. He says to Jack,

'Take a wee sup o' that!' It was like a dye bottle, about that size.

And Jack said, 'What is this for? Is it something to drink?'

'Never you mind,' said the wee man, 'you drink it!'

And Jack took one wee sup. The wee man snapped it oot o' his hand, put it back and put the cork on it, put it back in his belt. And lo and behold before you could say another word, Jack went like that . . . thiiiiiiist . . . he was the same size as the three wee elves!

'And now,' say the wee elves, 'ye're wir size. You come wi hus!' So the're two in the front, one behind. And they marched Jack off to Elfland. Down through this tunnel, through the ground and on, and on and on and on and on till they cam to the Elfin Palace. But afore they cam to the palace, Jack stopped them.

He said, 'Look, it's all right fir youse three,' he said, 'but I'm gettin awfa hungry. I never had nae meat today. My mother never gied me nae breakfast, and I've had a wee drink.'

'Oh, dinnae worry,' said the wee elf. 'When we land back at the king's palace, there's tae be meat for evermore. The're courses beyond reason! One course, two courses, three courses, four courses—you'll never eat aa the meat in the worl! We'll no go wi ye, Jack, no way. You walk into the palace, and sit doon,' he said. And this wee ane took off his hat and he put it on Jack's head. He said, 'You tak my hat and ye'll no be distinguished fae the rest o' them. But we'll no be far awa, we'll be listenin, we'll be oot o' earshot. But we'll still be there. But walk up to the palace and gae in—we'll show you whaur to go and sit doon at the table. And dinnae take yir hat off! Keep it on. And ye'll never be recognised.' This was Jack! 'But,' he said, 'mind, Jack, all the dinner comes in courses. It comes in one, two and three and four. And you remember, dinnae eat too much the first time, because the're plenty mair to come!'

So they showed Jack the hall door o' the kitchen. Jack

123

walks up and he comes into this great big room. And the're
a big monster table sittin in the middle, and these wee
people are sittin roond. The're a big high chair over in the
corner. This place was a cavern, a great big cavern. And
all these wee people are sittin roon. Jack walks in, he sits
doon. He keeps his hat doon, they tellt him to keep his
hat doon on his eyes, see! This hat was like a petal o'
a flooer—did ye ever see a blue-bell, a heather bell with
scallops round the throat? And Jack kept this blue-bell petal
ower his hair. And he sat doon at the table. Naebody paid
attention. In walks the king! And he sits doon at the high
chair, higher than all the others. It was a roond table and all
these wee people were sittin roon aboot. There were females
and males o' all description, but no children. They're all
sittin doon.

So the king claps his hands, clap, clap! And in comes the
first cook wi a big tureen full o' beautiful food. And he places
it on the table.

Jack bein hungry, he rubs his hands and he says out loud,
'That's ane o' them!'

The cook is upset. He goes back to the kitchen, he says,
'Look, we're fand oot!' There were four cooks in the kitchen.
He says, 'We're fand oot!'

'What do ye mean?' the second one says.

The chief cook said, 'We're fand oot. Ane o' them kens
what we've done.'

'Well,' the second cook says, 'they're busy eatin the noo.'
So Jack's sittin at the table and he's eatin up. Naebody pays
attention tae him, see! He's sittin fillin hissel. wi the best o'
the thing. And the table is cleared. In comes the next course,
the second cook places the thing doon.

Jack rubbed his hands thegither. He's hungry, he said,
'That's the second ane!' He meant the haben!

Back goes the second cook. 'Yes, definitely,' he says, 'I
dinnae ken hoo they fand . . . there's ane o' the elves kens
aa aboot us.'

'Well,' the third cook says, 'I'll bring in the salad.' So the third cook goes in wi the salad and he puts it on the table.

And Jack rubs his hands thegither, he says, 'That's the third ane!'

Back goes the cook to the kitchen. He says, 'We're done! We're done fir evermore! He knows everything. He's bound to ken. If he tells the king, we ken we're done.'

'Well,' the fourth cook said, 'there's only one left.' So he brought in the coffee, or the tea, whatever it was. The fourth ane placed it on the table.

And Jack rubbed his hands thegither, he said, 'Thank God, that's the last ane!' He was kind o' full noo, he said, 'Thank God, that's the last ane!'

Back goes the last cook. He says, 'Look, boys, it's finished. He kens the lot!'

'Well, look,' one says, 'get him in here! Try and steal him awa! Get him in here.'

So one o' the cooks goes oot to lure Jack into the kitchen. They tell Jack, 'Look, we ken who ye are! Ye're human, ye're no an elf like hus. You cam here tae tell on hus. What can we give you, ye winnae tell the king?'

Jack said, 'Wait a minute, ye must be mixed up or something. I'm no talkin aboot nothing. I cam in here tae have a good feed.'

'Whaur dae ye come fae?' one asked.

'Oh,' Jack says, 'I dinnae ken whaur I cam fae, but I cam in here fir a feed!'

He said, 'You ken we stole the king's treasure! And you ken we put it in a copper pot. And you ken us four cooks are guilty. You were gaunnae tell the king!'

'Oh, wait a minute,' says Jack. 'Is that what's it aboot? Well, I'll tell ye one thing, that's what I cam fir. I cam aboot this. And if ye're guilty, ye're gaunnae fit the punishment.' And just like that in come the three drunken elves tae Jack, in through the door.

125

He says, 'Jack, you finally fand the culprits. Ye fand the culprits!'

Jack said, 'Aye, I fand the culprits. That's them, the're four o' them. They've got the king's treasure that youse were blamed on when youse were guards o' the king's treasure. They stole it and they have it in a copper pot in the corner.'

So the three drunken elves gang over and lift the lid o' the copper pot. And sure enough there was the king's treasure the four cooks had stolen. 'Come on, Jack,' he says, 'come wi me.'

So the three drunken elves and Jack marched up in front of the king. And the king was sittin back noo by this time, after his dinner, ye see! And the three drunken elves bowed before their king. They said, 'Our majesty, we have returned.'

And the king said, 'I thought I banned youse away from Elfland fir evermore, because you were my three guards. And you guarded my treasure and it was stolen!'

'But wait a minute,' say the three drunken elves, 'our lord, would you forgive us, our majesty? You said that if we could bring a mortal back from earth who would tell us who had stolen the treasure, that all would be forgiven!'

'Yes,' said the king, 'I said that.'

'Well,' he said, 'we have brocht oot a mortal back from earth.'

So the king turned around, 'Yes,' he said, 'I made that promise, and I would like that mortal brought before me!'

So Jack was brought before the king. And Jack was very humbled before the Elfin King, because he had never before been before a king. And Jack was offered anything under the sun, and Jack couldnae speak, he was tongue-tied. So the little elves spoke up.

The king said, 'This mortal must be rewarded for his great work to me!'

And the little three elves said, 'Our majesty, all the mortal would like is one of your little barrels.'

126

'Take it, and take him with you,' he said. *'And may the luck and the wealth go with him for evermore!'*

So Jack was led off by the three drunken elves . . . Then all in a moment Jack wakened up and he rubbed his eyes. He thought to himself he had been asleep. And he rubbed his eyes again. He looked beside him and he saw this little barrel, and he says, 'I wonder what's in it.' He shaked it. It was full of something. And he took a drink . . . and he felt a *glow* passin down through his chest and down through his body. His head became light as a feather. And he picked up the barrel and he walkit home tae his mother.

His mother says, 'Where have you been, Jack? Where have you been these last two-three days?'

'Mother,' he said, 'I've not been nowhere for the last two-three days.'

She says, 'Jack, you've been gone for five days.'

'Mother,' he said, 'I only fell asleep on the moor for a couple o' minutes.'

And she says, 'What's that you've got?'

He says, 'Mother, nothing. Just a little barrel.' And he placed it on the mantelpiece.

His mother looked at it. 'Jack, if I'm no far mistaken,' she said, 'that is the same barrel that I saw many many years before your father. And I hope it disna do the same to you as it done to your father!'

'No, Mother,' he says, 'this is the barrel that'll keep me i' contentment for the rest of my life.' And it did keep him i' contentment for the rest of his life. An' ladies and gentlemen, that is the last of my story!

BEGGAR'S ISLAND

Now in all my collection of Jack stories the're many wonderful tales. When I was travelling walking the roads and working here and there as a young unmarried lad, I came across a group of travellers in Aberdeenshire away back in 1946 or 1947. And we had a storytelling session and I was asking about Jack stories. This old traveller man sitting by the fireside there was called Hector Kelby, and he told us this—the most intriguing story I've ever heard in all my life.

Jack lived with his mother a long time ago in a wee tumble-down house that his father left him. Ach, his father hadna been much of a man, much of a worker. He let things go to seed, ye know, and the wee bit croft that they had, father never paid much attention tae it. But we dinnae have much talk about his father, it's mostly about Jack and his mother. His mother had been good to Jack since he was a wee baby, and she brought him up and taught him all the things he knew. She told him all the stories in the evenings when there were little else to do. She worked hard for him. He took a wee few jobs along with farmers near the place where they lived. And he and his mother tried to survive the best they could. Jack was the age of eighteen when my story begins.

In the summer evenings Jack would always sit out on the doorstep of the little tumble-down cottage after the supper was over. And he'd be staring away out in the hills, staring away out in the mountains, staring out in the forest. And his mother would be busy washing the wee bit o' rags that they owned for clothes and making a wee bit food that she could afford for them.

And she'd always come out and sit down by his side when things were finished and say, 'Jack, what's troubling ye?'

'Well, Mother,' he said, 'I'm just thinking, out there is a world. The're a world I've never seen.' She'd told him many stories about things, about kings, about castles, princesses and stories that she'd heard as a child herself. And Jack had a longing deep in his heart. Oh, of course he had loved his mother. He loved to stay with his mother. But he had a longing in his heart to get out there and find the world for himself. So this one evening as the sun was setting, as usual Jack was sitting on the doorstep o' the tumble-down cottage, with the little thatched roof. Barns were falling down, an' they had a couple o' goats and two-three chickens scratching about.

She said, 'Laddie, what's troubling you?'

'Mother,' he said, 'look, I've made up my mind.'

She says, 'What hae you made up yir mind aboot, Jack?'

He says, 'Mother, I want to go oot in the world and look for a decent job to mysel, see a bit o' the world for mysel.'

'Oh, laddie, laddie,' she says, 'ye cannae go awa and leave me! What's about me, I'm my poor sel here. And you want to go oot in the world. Can you no gang around some o' the farms roond aboot the district?'

'Mother,' he said, 'I've worked all the farms, and I'm no happy at what I'm daein. I want to go farther into the world and see all these things you were tellin me aboot in your stories.'

But they argued and bargued with each other for a wee while. But at last the mother said, 'Well, laddie, if yir mind's made up, you want tae gae into the world. But look, it disna matter where ye gang, or whaur you be or where ever ye are, ye never forget about yir auld mother!'

He says, 'No, Mother, I'll no forget about you. I promise

you, Mother. I'll no be gone for too long. I jist want tae gae into the world and see the world for myself.'

So the next morning he got up, and she made him a wee bit breakfast. She fried him a wee collop and she baked him a wee bannock to carry him on his way. 'Well, Jack, laddie,' she said, 'it disna matter whaur ye are, never forget yir auld mother!'

'Mother,' he said, 'I'll never forget ye!' So he put his arms round his mother, he gave her a wee cuddle. And off he set.

Now Jack was on his way. The birds were singing, the sun was shining and Jack was going out into the world to seek his own fortune. So on he travelled. He travelled on and travelled on and on. In these days few and far between were the towns and villages a long time ago. Little crofts in the hills and wee toy thatched villages, but Jack passed through them all. He travelled on. But by mid-day he sat down and ate the wee bit bannock his mother had baked for him and his wee bit collop that she had fried for him on this way. 'That's it,' he says. 'God knows where the next is comin fae.' But he travelled on, on and on he travelled. That night he slept in an old tumble-down barn. And the hoolets were sitting, 'cahoo-oo-oo' in the barn! 'Cahoo'. Jack loved the noise o' the hoolets and their lonely sound.

But the next morning he got up bright and early. He'd slept sound that night. No breakfast. He went to a wee brook and got a drink o' water. And he travelled on his way. But then, the wee toy villages and the houses begint to disappear. And the forest begint to take over. The old road went through a forest and seemt to go on for ever and ever. And Jack travelled on. But during that day when the sun was high in the sky Jack got hungry. He would have eaten anything. He went to a wee burn looking for a wee trout he could guddle, although he didn't have matches or anything. He looked for rabbits or anything that would do along the roadside. But there was nothing. And then, he came to the end of the wood. Jack thanked God, 'Praise to God,' as the travellers would say, it was the end o' the wood. Now maybe there was somebody living here!

But he came to a wee clearing and the very first thing he saw was a wee toy house, a wee thatched house by the wayside. Jack said, 'There's somebody in here. I wonder wha's in here. Maybe there's an auld roadman, maybe an old farmer, an old crofter or somebody.'

But when he came round to the front of the wee old house, the first thing he saw was an old woman. And she was down on her knees. She was looking among the grass on her hands and knees and her back was to Jack. On her hands and knees in the grass, she was going through the grass. And Jack came up behind her for a wee while. He stopped behind the old woman. He could see that her black-grey hair was down her back. And she was dressed in an old ragged dress. The heels o' her boots were sticking out behind her. And Jack looked down upon the old woman, and he said, 'God bless my soul and body, what's gaun on here?'

And the old woman heard him. She turned round. And, brother, when the old woman turned round, her two eye holes were empty! She had no eyes! And Jack was . . . I don't know what like Jack felt for the woman, to look into her—first face he'd ever seen in his life with no eyes, just the bare eye holes!

And she knew by Jack's voice, she said, 'Laddie, laddie, laddie, would you help me, laddie, would you help me?'

An' Jack said, 'God bless my soul, old woman, what's wrong wi ye?'

She said, 'It's my only ee, my only ee I've got. It's lyin in the grass and I cannae get it. Would ye help me?'

'God bless us,' said Jack. What had happened? How can an old woman's eye fall out on the grass? Jack had never come across anything like this before in his life. But they looked among the grass, and the old woman was beating down the grass with her hands. And about two yards out from the old woman he saw this bloody red thing lying among the grass. It was an eye. And he picked it up tenderly in his fingers. It felt wet and slippery in his hand, it was an eyeball, a human eye.

He said, 'I've got it, old wife, I've got it, old wife, I've got it!'

'Oh laddie, laddie, give me it, put it in my hand!' she said.

And Jack reached over, and he put the eye in the old woman's hand.

And she catcht it, 'Oh God bless ye, son, God bless ye!' And she held it in her hand for a wee while. She held it close to her face for a while. And then she looked up. She closed it and she opened it a wee while. And the other eye closed . . . blank. And there was ae big blue eye sitting, one eye in her cheek. And Jack looked into her eye, big blue eye.

'Laddie, laddie,' she said, 'laddie, laddie, ye done that for me. I'll never forget ye!'

But he said, 'Old woman, what's wrang, what happened? What's wrang wi ye? What . . . I've never seen nothing like this before.'

'Laddie,' she said, 'come with me!' The wee house was just not far from where they were. And the door was open. Hens were running about, smoke was coming from the wee stone chimney. 'Come,' she said, 'come wi me.' She rushed into the wee house and within minutes she had the kettle on the old fire, the peats in the fire and the kettle on. She said, 'What's your name?'

He said, 'My name is Jack.'

'Jack,' she said, 'Jack!' She repeated it three times. So she wouldna forget it, 'Jack,' she says. 'I'll remember that.' Within minutes the old woman had the old kettle boiling and she took a big bowl. She put the pot o' tea and the big bowl on the table, and she gave Jack a bowl o' tea.

Now Jack was wondering what happened to this old woman

that her eye should fall out. Jack couldna believe this was true, a true story. It couldna fall out.

She says, 'Laddie, you've done an awfa thing for me!'

He said, 'I never did nothing for you, old woman. I only picked yir ee up frae the grass—onybody would hae done that for you.'

She says, 'Jack, where are ye gaun tae?'

Well Jack tellt her, 'I left my mother two days ago. I'm fed up bidin wi my mother, an' I want to see a wee bit o' the world.'

'Oh aye,' she said, 'laddie, ye want to see a wee bit o' the world, aye. *Well,*' she said, '*may the long roads and the twisted roads and the narrow roads and the wide roads take care o' ye as far as ye go. And you helped me and I'll help you.*'

But Jack sat there after he had his tea. He saw he couldna bide with the old woman. He was going to go on his way. 'Well, old woman,' he said, 'I must thank you for the tea.'

'Laddie, you helpit me,' she says, 'I'm gaunna help you!' And she went through a wee door in her house. She came back in a wee minute later and she said, 'Laddie, look, I want to gie you something. And I want you to tak it with ye. Because this is the cause o' me losin my ee!' She put on the table, brother, a pair o' scissors wi deer-horn handles, mounted with deer horn. With silver blades on them, the most beautiful pair o' scissors. Now Jack had seen many scissors with his mother back in his house, because she was an old woman who liked to sew. But Jack had never seen anything like this in all his life. The handles were made of deer horn, there were bonnie stones in them and they had silver blades. They were the most beautiful things in the world.

But Jack wondert, 'What is the old woman puttin this on the table for?'

She said, 'Jack, ye see that lyin there? That's the cause o' me losin my ee.'

But Jack said, 'Why should that lose yir ee?'

133

She said, 'Listen, I'll tell ye a wee story. My father, God rest him, workit for a magician a long time ago. And my father was awfae clever. And these scissors were the magician's scissors, and that magician could do anything with these scissors. My father stole them fae him, and he brought them here to this hoose. And he gave them to me. For years I've promised my father I would never part with them and never give them up. That magician has penalised me all his life—he's tooken my leg and he's thrawn it in the grass where I couldna find it. He's tooken my arm, he's tooken my ee . . . And it was lucky that you cam by that I was able to get my ee back. Or I would never hae found it. All because he wants his scissors back.'

But Jack says, 'What's so important about that? They're only a pair o' shears. My mother . . .'

'No these, Jack, they're different. And noo, Jack, you're gaun into the world, Jack, and I want ye tae do something for me. I want you to take them with ye. And then,' she says, 'they'll be gone! And he'll no penalise me nae mair.'

But Jack said, 'What are they for?'

'I'll tell ye,' says the old woman, 'what they're for, Jack!' She says, '*Look, onything you want in this world, you can clip into the air and ask for it, and you'll get it.* And I want you to take them oot o' my life, so he'll never penalise me again. Noo, tak them with ye! And if ye ever are in trouble and ye ever want onything, just keep them in your pocket. But dinnae use them unless you have to.' And she closed the scissors and she gave them to Jack.

Jack put them in his pocket, the beautiful scissors. There were deer-horn handles and all these precious looking stones in them, and silver blades, the most beautiful pair o' scissors Jack had ever seen in his life. So Jack thought the old woman was kind o' queer. But he put them in his pocket anyway and he thanked the old woman.

She said, 'Thank ye, God, son, and thank ye, God, Jack, for takkin them oot o' my life! Noo, the magician'll never bother me again when I tell him the truth they're gone for ever.'

Anyway, Jack accepted the scissors from the old woman. And he bade good-bye and on he went. He travelled on his way. But with the scissors in his pocket, he never gave the old woman another thought. On his way here, he lay there in barns, he lay in sheds, and he worked here and he worked there to farmers, and he got a wee taste o' money. He went into the wee village and he had a wee glass o' beer on his travels. A wee drink here and lying there. But in his pocket o' his old coat were still his scissors. He was always asking, 'Whaur is the big toon?' to everybody he came to.

'Oh,' the people would say, 'there's nae a big toon here, Jack, ye'll have to go further on.'

But he travelled on and travelled on and travelled on. But now his beard begint to grow. And his coat begint to get torn. Jack had been on the road now for nearly three months. And he got a wee bit . . . without a wash, without a shave, he got like a real beggarman, though he was a good, young handsome man. But he travelled on. At last, late one night he came to where he saw the lights of a great big town. Flares, it wasna lights, out in the street. 'Oh,' he says, 'a big toon!' What they would call a big town was a large village. 'But,' he says, 'I'm no gaun intae it tonight.' So he kept up in the wee shed beside a big peat stack. An' he fell asleep with his coat over his head. But in the morning he said, 'I'll gang into the toon!'

He walked down to the town. And he could see there was a high hill, and a big castle sitting on the hill, a big palace. There was a village and all the people about, and farms out in the country. Oh, it was a real big town in old bygone days. And Jack was just walking down the street wondering where he was going to, when all in a moment out came two-three guards with their spears and their shields! And Jack was arrested. Half a dozen o' them! The're two took his arm, and two went in back with spears at his

135

back. And he was led down through the village to a pier, a quay.

Jack said, 'I' the name of the world . . .' He asked the question, but they never spoke to him. Guards with helmets on their heads, spears and shields led him down to the pier. There was a lake, a big loch by the side o' the town. And there was a boat on the lake. Jack was bustled aboard the boat, two guards at the back, two guards at the front, two guards in the middle. And Jack was rowed out for about half a mile into this big lake. And when they rowed him out to the middle o' the lake, there was an island. But there were not trees on this island, it was just cut bare! He was thrown overboard, thrown on to his hands and knees on the gravel o' the island. And the boat pulled away back to the village. Jack could see the boat.

Jack said, 'I' the name o' God, what am I daein here? What, what have I done?' But there was nobody to argue with. He walked up to the middle of the island. And there were dozens of people—old men with torn coats, an' they had long beards and skinny faces. There were women and children and they were all so poor and naked and skinny. Jack said, 'I' the name o' God, why am I here?' And he looked all about— they had wee huts built wi bits o' stick, and wee huts built wi branches. Jack could see that everybody was no better than beggars.

But there was one old man who stepped out in front o' the crowd. He said, 'Welcome, son, welcome, son, welcome, son. Welcome tae Beggar's Island.' And he took Jack up to a clearing where they'd built a bing o' huts, huts made o' branches. This was their village, this was Beggar's Island.

Now, the king in the town had passed a law that no beggars or vagrants were allowed in his town in any way. Anyone who was a vagrant or a beggar was arrested immediately who came into the town and put aboard the boat and sent to the island. This was where the king put all the beggars—on Beggar's Island. And there they lived in starvation and poverty. The only food they got was two times a week, a boat came with the big pots from the palace where they boilt the porridge for the soldiers and for everybody in the palace. And they scraped the pots. That's all the beggars got—the scrapings o' the porridge pots two times a week. Anybody found in the town who was a vagrant or a beggar was shipped across to the island and there they were left. They could live as they liked on this island. There was water on the island, but nothing else. There were no trees. The king had given orders all the trees had to be cut so that they couldna make rafts to escape. And beggar after beggar was put on the island. They were starving, they were hungry, they were naked, they were poor, they were swarming with lice. They were down-to-earth people who the king thought were just not fit to be in his kingdom. And this is where Jack was put by the guards on the boat.

So the old man walked up, 'Welcome, son, welcome! Another traveller, another poor beggar.' Now Jack looked the part with his torn coat and his torn trousers and his boots worn. His beard and his hair had never been washed or combed for many days. Jack was only about nineteen years old, a young handsome man. But he was classed as a beggar along with the rest of them.

So they were gathered together, and what they were doing— they had a fire and they were roasting earthnuts! You know, the pig-nuts you dig out of the ground, the earthnuts. They were roasting them and this old woman says, 'Tak two or three, laddie, tak two-three. It'll do you good. It's all ye're gaunna get till the porridge pots come. It'll no be for the rest of the week yet, before the pots come, twice a week frae the king's castle.' The scrapings of the pots he delivered to the island, the brochan, came in the boats. And they used to dive among it with their hands and eat it, you know, they were starving. But that was the first day. Jack hadna much to eat that day because he saw the wee bairns were starving, the old folk were starving.

137

Everybody was hungry waiting for the porridge pots to come.

So the next evening Jack sat down by the fire with all these beggars, wee hungry children, old people sitting there starving and naked roasting earthnuts on the fire. Jack sat there beside them, he was one of them. And then he thought, 'Why am I here? Why did I leave my mother in the first place?' And then he thought about his mother, and then he thought about his travels, he thought about the old woman whose eye had fallen on the grass. And then . . . he remembert the scissors that the old woman had given him. The scissors of the magician who had penalised the old woman. Jack thought, 'I'd better work . . . try and see.' So he put his hand in his pocket. Now his pocket was worn, and the scissors dropped down into the lining. But reaching down into the lining of his pocket, Jack brought up the scissors, the most beautiful scissors you ever saw in all your life. Deer-horn handles, polished and shiny with precious stones, silver blades, the most beautiful little pair o' scissors Jack had ever seen. The old woman had said, 'If you ever want anything . . .' And Jack looked all around. There were the wee bairns eating the skins. Some people were roasting earthnuts on the ground and throwing wee bits o' skins, and the wee craturs were running with their wee fingers picking them up. And Jack felt so sad about this.

He took the scissors and he said, 'If this really works, old woman,' he said, 'I wish we had some food!' And he clipped the scissors in the air. And lo and behold, brother, as soon as he clipped the scissors and asked for some food, ye never saw nothing like this in the world! Within the front o' him, there was a cloth laid on the ground, and all the food in the world was laid before him! Roasted legs of chicken, roasted legs of meat, and everything that they ate in these bygone days was laid before him. And the people around stared in amazement. They rushed forward and one by one as Jack kept clipping and kept clipping and kept clipping the air, then the food came in loads. Food of all description. The people rushed to it, they ate it and they tore it with their hands, they were so excited. Till everyone ate to their heart's content, they couldna eat another bite. There was more stuff left on the cloth that would feed an army. The wee weans were lying with their bellies full, holding their hands on their stomachs. The old men were lying on their sides, they couldna eat another bite. And the old women were sitting chewing on bones. Jack never saw so much food in all his life!

And they all went over and said to him, 'Laddie, laddie i' the name o' God, whaur in the world did ye come fae? Where in the world did ye get all the food?' An' Jack looked around, they were all in rags.

Jack said, 'Well, now they had food, we've got to give them something to dress theirsel with!' So he clip-clip-clip and he asked for clothes of all description. And then the garments fell in dozens, the most beautiful garments, shawls for the old women, trousers for the old men and clothes for the weans. Jack kept clipping, asking for . . . and soon there was a heap of clothes as big as a mountain. And they were rushing in and putting on all these fancy clothes, they were dressing theirsels. As fast as Jack could clip, as fast as the clothes were falling, the weans and the women were rushing forward. Till every woman was dressed, till they couldna dress theirsels anymore! And still there was plenty left.

And then, all the people gathered round Jack. And every one, every one wanted to put their hands on him at the same time. 'Wait, wait,' says Jack, 'wait a minute, wait a minute!'

So the old man in the village says, 'Laddie, laddie, where in the world did you come from? What have ye brought tae us?'

And Jack said, 'I've brought you this!' And he held up the wee pair o' shears. Every one was dressed in the finest clothes. Everybody had meat they could eat! Now Jack looked around the village and he seen that there were wee hovels

139

they had made with branches, made with straw and things they had collected around the island, made with grass. And he says, 'That's nae guid!' So Jack went up and he asked for a hut, and he asked for a house, and he asked for a house, and another one, another one, another one, and he kept clipping. And the more he asked for the more . . . soon there was a beautiful wee village on the island. Better houses than there were in the town. Till everyone had everything they needed. So Jack was the hero of the day. They, the old people, wouldna let him out o' their sight.

So next day, in comes the king's guards from the town with the boat, with the big porridge pots. So all the elders and the headman of the village say, 'Look, Jack, what's coming!'

Jack said, 'What is it?'

He said, 'That's them coming with their porridge pots.'

Jack said, 'We're no needing their porridge pots, are we?'

'No,' he says, 'but we'll teach them a lesson.'

So down go the old men dressed in the finest of finery, beautiful cloaks and beautiful coats and swords hanging by their sides. And when the boat came in, they pulled the boat, and they catcht the guards, they dooked them in the porridge pots heid first! And rubbed them with porridge and stuck them in the pots, and said, 'Go back to your master and tell the king we need nothing from ye!' Two o' the men that they left to row the boat were very lucky. They got away without getting rubbed in the porridge because they were needing to row the boat.

So when the six guards rowed back to the mainland to the palace, they rushed up. First thing they met was the captain of the king's guards. 'Well,' said the captain, 'did ye feed the beggars?'

'Beggars!' he said. 'Feed the beggars? We never fed the beggars. The beggars are no needin fed. The beggars are dressed in the finest o' finery!' They were led before the king. They told the king the whole story. They said, 'The

140

beggars, my lord, the're houses in the village better than wir own. The beggars are dressed in the most finery in the world. And they're not needing any food, they need nothing!'

The king said, 'This is impossible, this couldna happen. That's Beggar's Island, that's where all my vagrants go.'

'Not anymore,' say the guards. 'We want never to go back there again. They're standing there dressed like noblemen with swords, and they rubbed us in the porridge and sent us back in the boat. Oh, master, please don't send us back!'

The king was upset about this. So next day he sent ten soldiers to the island. The same thing happened. The ten soldiers were sent back again. Anyway, the king got very upset.

He says, 'What's happening out there? What has happened?' And the king had two beautiful daughters, an older one and a younger one. The queen had died, and they lived with their father the king.

The older one said, 'Father, Father, if you're so upset, let me go out tomorrow in the boat! Let me see what's troubling you. Dress me as a beggar and I'll go to the island and see what's happening.' So the oldest princess went to the island. She got the oldest coat she could get, and dressed herself in rags. And she got one of the men to row her across to the island and fling her off the boat.

The chief guard flung her off the boat and she crawled on her hands and knees. The first person she crawled up to, there was standing a young handsome nobleman dressed in the beautiful cloth, head to foot and a sword hanging by his side. And he'd watched her coming from the boat.

'Welcome,' he said, 'welcome, my dear, welcome. Poor beggar woman, welcome.' And he led her up and took her into one of the cottages where there was food galore. There was food in every cottage, for Jack had given everyone as much as they could eat. 'Sit down there, my dear, and have something to eat.'

Now the princess, the king's oldest daughter, looked all

141

around. She was wanting to find out what was happening on this island, to get all the information for her father the king. But as you know, in these bygone days they didna have any tables and chairs in houses, because they werena required, they werena even thought of. And everybody only ate their food from the ground, on the floor. So Jack took it in hand to see the young woman, like the rest of the people, should be fed. He clipped the scissors and he spread a napkin on the floor. All these beautiful things were set on the floor for her to eat.

But being a princess, because the things were lying on the floor, she said, 'I could not eat that, I couldn't eat off the floor. No one eats off the floor.'

'Well,' he said, 'my dear, if you can't eat off the floor . . . us beggars eat off the floor, and we're content. You're not a beggar. You're a spy!' So he took her and he made her confess. And she said she was the king's daughter. 'Well,' he said, 'the king's daughter tomorrow'll go back in the porridge pot!'

So the next day when the pots came in, when the boat came in to try and deliver porridge from the palace, Jack took her down with the help o' some o' the men from the island. They put the princess into the porridge pot and they rubbed her, covered her over with the scrapings and sent her back to the king. When she crawled back to her father the king covered in porridge from head to foot from the pot, with bits o' tatties and sausages or whatever they had in the pot covered on her head, she was crying. The tears were running down her cheeks.

She said, 'Oh, Daddy, why'd you send me there? Why did you send me?'

He said, 'I thought you were going out to find the truth!'

She says, 'I couldn't find anything bad, I couldn't find anything. Please, please forgive me!' And she was rushed off to her room to tidy herself up.

So that night in the palace there was a meeting of the king

and all his councillors. The king said, 'I want to know the truth what's going on out on that island!'

So the youngest daughter said, 'Daddy, let me go. I'll find the truth.'

But he says, 'You'll only end up like your sister.'

'No, Daddy,' she says, 'I'll no end up like my sister.' She was a wee bit more clever, a wee bit more intelligent than her sister.

So the next morning the king finally gave consent. The younger sister was rowed across on the boat with the porridge pots. But the same thing happened as before. The beggars cowped the porridge pots and flung them into the sea. Everyone was dressed like bene hantle. They were like ladies and gentlemen walking about the island! And they needed no porridge pots from the king. They chased the soldiers for their life. They threw the princess on the shore dressed in rags. And Jack was standing there smiling away, watching the young lassie crawling up on her hands and knees from the shoreside where the guards had thrown her.

'Come, my dear,' he said, 'you're welcome, you're one of us!' Her hair was hanging down over her, wet with the water from the shore. Her coat was in rags and she looked the real part. But she was the youngest daughter of the king! He led her up and to the first cottage. He said, 'Are you hungry, my dear?'

'Oh,' she said, 'I'm starving! I'm starving, I wish I had something to eat.'

And Jack said, 'Well, you'll have something to eat!' And he clipped like that with the scissors. And there was a beautiful cloth laid on the floor of the little cottage where Jack lived, and all these goodies were put on the floor. She got down on her hands and knees and she was eating, eating, feeding on her hands and knees. And Jack looked, Jack knew this was no fake. This was the original. And so she and Jack got to be good friends. Jack fed her for two days, he fed her for three days, he fed her for four days. But she never

143

mentioned anything. She walked round the island, she saw all the people dressed in their finery. The houses were full of food, the houses were lovely, the children were happy and the children were playing.

And she says, 'Young man . . .'

And he said, 'Nae young man! My name is Jack!'

'But,' she says, 'Jack, where in all the world did all this come from?'

By this time Jack begint to take a fancy to this young woman, ye see! He liked her a lot. 'Well,' he said, 'my dear, it's a long story.' So one evening as they sat by the shoreside o' the little island while the sun was setting, Jack told her the story, how he'd left his mother a long time ago and how he'd been lucky to come to an old woman who had lost her eye and how she gave him her scissors, and how he'd come to Beggar's Island. Jack told the whole story.

'Well,' she said, 'look, I'm a beggar—but it's a mistake why I'm here. You see, my father is a rich man.'

But Jack said, 'If yir father's a rich man, why are you here?'

'Well,' she said, 'it's all a mistake. You see, I had a good friend o' mine and she was very poor. I changed clothes with her just so that she could go and have something to eat in my father's house. And I was arrested just like you and I was put to the island. And I want you, Jack, to come and meet my father.'

Now Jack begint to feel a little affection for this young woman, and he thought. 'Well,' he said, 'I'll go and meet your father if that's what you want.'

So next morning he called a council for all the people in the village. They all came together from the little houses he'd got for them. He said, 'Look, I'm gaunna give youse all the food youse want. And I'm gaunna give youse all the clothes you want.' And Jack clipped the shears and created a great big barn. He filled the barn with all the clothes they would ever need. And he filled the barn with all the food

144

they would ever need. 'Now,' he said, 'I'm going back to the mainland.'

And all the people of the island gathered around him and said, 'Please, don't go! Please don't go, don't leave us!'

But Jack said, 'I have to go. I must.' Everyone was sad to see Jack going. But he said, 'I must go.'

So the next day when the boat came in with the porridge pots, as usual they put the porridge over the side of the boat. And Jack commanded that he and the young woman should be taken over to the mainland. When Jack and the young woman were taken to the mainland, the first thing that met him was five guards with their spears. And he was led before the king.

Jack turned to the young woman and he said, 'You have deceived me! I thought you went . . .'

She said, 'This is my father. Jack, here is my father— the king.' So Jack was led into a little room. And the princess in a minute just nicked away through a door and she came back dressed in a beautiful gown. Jack looked in amazement. He saw the young princess and he knew he'd been deceived.

He says, 'Young woman, you have deceived me.'

She said, 'This is my father the king!'

And the king sat there and he said, 'Now, young man! Tell me, what's been going on there? That's my Beggar's Island. And you have fed these people, you've clothed these people more than I could afford. Why is it that you did that for all these people?'

'Well,' Jack said, 'my lord, my king, to tell ye the truth, I'm just a poor young man and I was very lucky to fall in with an old woman who gave me something special. She gave me a pair of scissors, and I can clip anything I want.'

King wouldna believe this. 'Then clip something for me, young man!'

Jack said, 'What would you like, my lord?'

He said, 'Young man, for the peril of your life—if this is

145

wrong, your head shall be tooken from your body! Clip me a gown!'

And Jack took the beautiful scissors from his pocket. He clipped up in the air, and there fell the most beautiful gown of all the beautiful colours in the world. And the king stood in amazement. Jack said, 'Put it on, my lord!'

And the king threw off his cloak. He put on this beautiful gown that Jack had clipped from the air. He says, 'Young man, this is magic! This is magic beyond understanding!'

'Well,' Jack said, 'my lord, you see, I had to take care o' these people, my lord. They might be beggars, my lord, but they're just human beings like you and I. They're people. And I had no other choice, I fed them and I took care of them.'

'Young man,' said the king, 'this is magic.' And there sat the princess in a beautiful dress. And Jack was fancying her. He looked at her and she was looking at him. The king says, 'Young man, what am I going to do with you?'

'Well,' Jack says, 'look, my lord. There's only one thing I would ask for your permission,' he said. 'I want to go back to my mother.'

'Your mother?' said the king.

Jack said, 'Yes, my lord. If you forgive me, my lord. I want to go back to my mother. I'll give you the scissors, if they're any use tae ye.'

The king took the scissors in his hand. He says, 'Is this the thing that all the trouble is about?' And he took them and clip-clip-clipped in the air . . . Nothing. Nothing happened. Not a thing happened. The king said, 'This is what all the trouble's about? I sent my daughter to the island? My beggars are dressed in clothes? And you sent my guards back and my porridge pots covered in porridge? All for this?' And he held up the scissors and he clip-clip-clipped in the air. And he said, 'And you got me a gown?' He clipped again. 'They're no good to me, young man,' said the king.

146

Jack said, 'Look, my lord, my king, only me can use these scissors.'

'Young man,' said the king, 'I see, eh, you want back to your mother?'

Jack said, 'Yes, I would love to see my old mother.' So Jack sat down and he told the king the whole story I'm telling you.

And the king turned round, he said, 'Young man, you're very clever. And you're very wise. You've done a lot of wonderful things I've never done. But now I'm beginning to realise I've made a big mistake.' He said, 'From now on, there'll be no more beggars on Beggar's Island!'

'Well,' Jack said, 'that's all I ask of you, my lord. I'll give you the scissors, I'll do anything for you. But you must get rid of all the beggars on Beggar's Island. There's no need to be beggars there, my lord,' he said. 'They're just people like you and I.'

'Well,' the king said, 'you've dressed them in finery and you've fed them. I don't see why they should be out there anymore. We'll bring them back to the town!'

So the next morning the king sent boats to the island to bring every one back to the town. 'But now, young man,' he said, 'I don't know what I'm going to do with you.'

Jack said, 'All I'm asking, my lord . . . you can have the scissors. I want to go back to my mother.'

And then the young princess got up. 'But,' she says, 'what about me, Jack? Don't you have any thought for me?'

And Jack said, 'Well, I have a little thought for you. In fact, I think a lot of you!'

'Well,' the king said, 'I tell ye what I'll have to do here. I need someone in my court to supply my whole castle with clothes. With gowns and clothes. And I see by the way I can't use your scissors . . .' He said, 'You try them, my dear!'

The princess took the shears. And she tried to clip in the air and ask for anything. But nothing happened.

'I see, young man,' he said, 'that you're the only one that

147

can use these things. And I need you. I need you a lot! You could dress all my palace for the rest of your life.'

But Jack said, 'I want to go back to my mother!'

And the king said, 'What age is your mother?'

Jack said, 'My lord, my king, my mother is an old woman and she's in rags. I've been gone for a long long time. I'd love to go home to my mother.'

And the princess looked, she said, 'Jack, would you like to take me with you to see your mother?'

Jack said, 'No, my dear, I couldna take you with me. My mother lives in a tumble-down cottage a long way from here. And she'll pro'bly by this time—she'll be in rags.'

And the king said, 'Nonsense, young man! If you could dress all my beggars on Beggar's Island, and dress them like noblemen,' he said, 'pro'bly you could dress your mother like a lady! So that me and my daughter could meet her!' And that is the end of my story.

JACK AND THE FARMER'S TREASURE

I remember away up in a place called Blantyre in Lanarkshire, an old uncle and a few o' us got together one night and we were campit beside an old pit bing. We were telling stories and discussing stories, Jack tales. So Uncle Sandy said, 'I'll tell ye a ghost story. Did ye ever hear a Jack ghost story?' I said, 'No, Uncle, I've heard many stories about Jack, but not many Jack ghost stories.' 'Well,' he said, 'this is one!' Where he heard it I cannae tell ye, because I've never heard anyone else tell it before. And I've heard stories from many sources. And his name was Sandy Reid, he was my mother's brother-in-law.

A long time ago there wonst lived a rich farmer away up in the West Highlands. And this farmer was very rich, he had the best stock, he had the best horses, he had the best cattle in the whole valley where he lived. Beside the valley where he lived there were a small village. And this was where all the farmers came on market day. Now beside his farm there were a small church, and in the church there were a small cemetery. In that cemetery was a tomb that belonged to the generation of this farmer. His grandfathers and his great-grandparents were all buried in this private tomb.

So he was middle-aged by the time he married and he married this young woman, half his age. Now he had many men workin for him. But he treated the young woman like a slave because the men that worked on the farm used to

149

report what he would do on her when they went to the toon
to talk in the pub and have a drink. He never took her to
church wi him, he never took her to market wi him. It was
just orderin her around the place! And the men who workit
wi him, maybe seven or eight men, they were fed up wi him
orderin the young woman aroond. She was dressed in rags,
he never bought her a decent dress, he bought her nothing.
And word soon got to the village. Now when he came to the
village he was always dressed in the best. When he went to
church he had the best carriage for going to church, he had
everything his heart desired. But he treated his poor young
wife like a slave.

And then one day for no reason atall, he sold all the best
cattle he had, he sold all the best sheep and he sold all the
best horses, and left very little on the farm. Then about four
days later he died. Oh, the people werena sorry when he died,
because he wasna a very nice person at any rate. But after
the funeral arrangements . . . now he was entombed where
his grandfather and grandmother were buried. He was in
the tomb there, and after the funeral passed people begint
to come up to the farmer's wife and ask for money. Because
he owed a lot of people in the village a lot o' money.

She tellt them, 'I've nae money.' He never left her a
penny. Whatever he'd done with his money nobody knew.
The blacksmith cam askin for money, the grocers cam askin
for money, people from the markets cam. But there were not
a penny in the hoose. So for to keep hersel alive she had tae
sell the rest o' the animals that were on the farm for to pay
her workers. But then, he had only been buried for a month
when strange things began to happen about the farm. Because
the workers began to say, the cattlemen, the shepherds and
the rest o' the men began to say—that the farmer's ghost was
walkin roon the farm. He could plainly be seen walkin roon
the farm at night! And naturally he scared them off.

So one by one the workers left with the fricht o' the ghost
o' the farmer comin back at night. Because everybody swore

they'd seen the farmer walkin roon the buildings, comin out o' the tomb and walkin around the farm steadings. So one by one, as I say, the workers left, till at last the poor woman was left by hersel. She was heartbroken, she didna know what to do. The only thocht she had, thing she could say was to sell the farm and move awa.

But it happened that who should come lookin for work but Jack. Jack had been travellin the valley goin from farm to farm lookin for work, and he had word that such and such a farm—men were leavin. And maybe he'd get the chance o' a job there. So when he came to the farm and he knocked on the door the young woman cam oot. And Jack bein a handsome good lookin young man, the young woman took an instant likin to him. And she invited him into the hoose for something to eat. And she explained to him.

She said, 'What's yir name?'

He said, 'My name's Jack.' And he said, 'I'm lookin fir work, any kind o' work, I'll do anything aroond the place.'

'Well,' she says, 'young man, I could do with you. Because there's plenty work to be done in this place. But I've nae money to pay ye.'

'But a farm this size,' he said, 'should always manage to be able to pay the workers.'

So she sat doon and tellt him the story about hoo her husband had been so miserable and how he'd hid his money— or what he'd done with the money nobody knew. How she owed people in the village, how she owed everyone. And how his ghost started to walk aboot. And one by one the workers began to move awa. She says, 'I could dae wi you, Jack.' She took a likin to Jack, because Jack was a young handsome man and she was only a young woman hersel!

And Jack says tae her, 'What is it that's scarin the folk awa?'

She says, 'My husband's ghost. He walks here every night at twelve o'clock. I've never seen him. But he's scared off the workers. Event the maid that used to work for me—she's

151

seen him and she's gone. And I'm left all alone. I could dae with your work, lad, but it's up tae yirsel. I've nae money tae pay ye.'

'Ah well,' Jack said, 'I'm no really broke yet. And I have a few shillings to keep me. And whatever I need . . . if ye'll give me a bit o' meat—'

'Oh,' she says, 'ye can have as much meat as ye can eat! Ye can eat with me!'

So Jack began to work at the farm. He did all the jobs about the place that was needin done. So that night he thought to himself, after the young woman had went to bed, 'I would like to see this ghost at's wannerin aboot.'

So he sat up till twelve o'clock, till the wee clock in the church struck twelve. And then he took a wanner roon the graveyard, a wanner roon the little tomb. It was covered in ivy. And in below the wee church . . . the hoolets were roarin on top o' the church. And the moon was passin by quick and the clouds darkened. Then he heard the skreek of an auld oak door o' the tomb. But he never stood up. He hid behind a gravestane in the wee churchyard! And he watched.

The door opened. And oot came an old fat farmer! As if he was just inside for a look. And he wannert roon the graveyard and he wannert roon the church. And Jack keeked here and there. He wannert roon the buildings and then he went back. Jack heard the skreekin o' the door, and the tomb door shut. 'Aha!' says Jack. 'It's him aa right! It's him aa right,' he says.

So the next morning after breakfast he says to the young widow-woman, 'I was wantin to take the day off the day.'

'Oh,' she says, 'Jack, if ye want to take the day off it's up to yirsel. You just dae what ye please about here.'

'I want to gang to the village,' he said. 'Are there a blacksmith in the village?'

'Oh aye, laddie,' she says, 'but ye canna go near him.'

He says, 'What wey?'

'Well,' she says, 'my man that dee'd, the farmer owes him

152

an awfa money. If you come fae this place he'll do naething for ye.'

'Ach,' he said, 'I'm just wantin a wee job done. And I have a bit money mysel, I'll manage tae pay him.' So he had a bit breakfast with the farmer's wife and awa he goes doon to the wee village. He hadna far to gang, maybe a mile's walk. And he soon cam to the blacksmith's shop. The busy old grey-heided blacksmith was chappin awa with his hammer wi his leather apron on, his back to the door. And the door was swung wide open. Jack walked in and said hello to the old blacksmith.

The old blacksmith turned round, 'Well, laddie,' he says, 'what can I dae for ye? Brought a horse alang?'

'No,' says Jack, 'I've brocht nae horse. I dinnae hae nae horses. But I'll pay ye well if ye could dae a wee job for me.'

'What kind o' job can I do, laddie?' he says. 'I'm no really busy the noo. And if ye hae a wee bit job, it'll aye be a help tae me.'

Jack said, 'I want ye to mak me an iron glove.'

'An iron glove?' he said. 'But what do ye want an iron glove fir? I've heard of iron gloves years ago when old knights were on the go. But the're nae need for iron gloves noo.'

'Well,' Jack said, 'I want you to mak me an iron glove.'

'Oh well,' he says, 'I might mak something that looks like an iron glove tae ye. But for perfection . . . it'll no be very good.'

Jack said, 'It'll no matter. And I want ye to mak me a breast plate, an iron breast plate.'

'A breast plate?' said the blacksmith. 'But what in the name o' God are ye gaunna do with a breast plate? The're nae need for that noo-a-days, laddie, that's hundreds o' years ago!'

Jack said, 'I want ye to mak me a plate wi a couple o' straps to go on my shouders, just tae haud it in place. And aboot three feet broad wi straps on the top to haud it on.'

'Oh well,' the old blacksmith said, 'I've never made things

like that tae folk before in my life. But if you're in the village for a wee while, give me some time. Come back in about an hour, and I'll see what I can do for ye.'

So Jack took a wander doon the village and into the wee inn and he had a glass o' beer. And he wandered aboot and he bocht two-three things that he thocht the farmer's wife would need, ye see. And he cam back. About two hours he was awa. The auld blacksmith was finished his work. And there lyin the top o' the bench was an iron glove, like a hand with fingers on it made o' iron. And Jack picked it up and he slipped his hand inside it. It wasna very well done, but Jack said it would dae the purpose.

'But in the name o' God,' said the blacksmith, 'what are ye gaunna dae wi that?'

'Ah,' Jack said, 'I have a wee job for it!'

And he says, 'There's yir plate, that was easy made. But the glove took a wee bit o' daein.'

Jack said, 'That's fine, the very things I need.' So he paid the auld blacksmith mair than he would ever need or should hae gien him. The auld blacksmith was pleased, ye see, wi the money!

So Jack picked them up, put them under his arm, and with the wee bits o' parcels he had bought for the farmer's wife, things he thought she would need, he wandered his way hame. But when he cam near the farm he didna tak the plate and the glove in the hoose. He reached ower and put them doon the back o' the graveyard. And he took the messages in to the farmer's wife, and he gied her the things that he bought for her and she was awfa pleased, ye see. She never got naebody tae buy a present in her life tae her!

So she made Jack something to eat and he dandered aboot the farm, daein wee bits o' jobs. He couldna wait till night would come. And then they sat and cracked a long long while, and the farmer's wife began to think an awful lot o' Jack. She began to like him an awful lot. And he liked her tae. So the farmer's wife went off to her bed.

And Jack sat a wee while longer, and he went into ane o' the bedrooms. He pulled a white sheet off ane o' the beds. White bedsheet. He rolled it up in a knot and put it under his oxter. He waited, the clock was just quarter to twelve in the hoose. And he walked oot to the graveyard. Roon to the back of the dyke, hand doon, and got the iron glove. And then he got the breast plate and he put the plate ower his shoulder with the two straps. He put the glove on his hand. And he wapped the white sheet aroon him! Then the clock on the old church struck twelve o'clock. And Jack went up behind the tombstone, as close as he could to the gate o' the tomb which was covered in ivy—it was an auld iron door!

And he heard click, skreek—the door opened. And oot comes the old farmer's ghost wonst again. When Jack saw the old farmer's ghost comin oot from the tomb he walked up. And he comes close as he could.

The ghost spoke, 'Who are you? Are ye one o' hus?'

Jack said, 'I am one o' youse!'

'If you're one o' us,' he said, 'let me feel your hand!' So Jack slipped the cauld hand oot fae below the white sheet he had wapped aroon him, the iron hand he had got made in the smiddie. And the old farmer reached oot and he catcht and he shook it. 'Aye,' he said, 'ye are one of hus! Whaur's yir hole?'

Jack said, 'At the back o' the dyke. I was a poor poor man, and they wouldna bury me in here, so they buried me near the side o' the dyke.'

'And what are ye daein oot here?' said the farmer. 'Ye know I'm on my travels roon my property.'

'Oh,' Jack said, 'I'm on my travels tae. I'm gaun up tae the hillside to coont my money.'

'Well,' the farmer said, 'I'll be gaun up tae the hillside tae coont my money! But I'll hae tae go for a wee wanner roon the place first. I'll see ye later!'

Jack said, 'Right-o!' Nae fricht, nae fear or nothing! Like that the farmer vanished away roon the barn doors.

155

Jack whipped off the white sheet aff him, got the breast plate and the glove and he rolled them in a knot, hid it in a wee corner o' the graveyard. And popped ower the dyke and back intae the farm hoose, went tae his bed. Never said a thing to the farmer's wife.

So the next morning he went oot after he had his breakfast and he went to the side of the graveyard. He got a spade and he dug a wee square like a grave beside the graveyard dyke. He didna dig very deep, but he covered it ower, it looked like a grave. The bare rouch sand, he made it in the shape of a grave. And then in to the farmer's wife.

He says tae her, 'I want ye tae gather me aa the coins ye have in the farm hoose. Ken, halpenies and pennies, aa the cheapest money you've got.'

But she says, 'Jack, what in the world are ye gaunna do wi them? I'll gie ye the last money I have. I'll gie ye a couple o' gold sovereigns if ye want tae go to the village.'

'No,' he says, 'I dinnae want gold sovereigns. I want aa the old, kind o' auld gold coins you've got.'

So the farmer's wife raiked roon the hoose and she gathered aa the pennies or halpenies, whatever kind o' coins they had in these bygone days, and she gied them to Jack.

So Jack took them in, he put them in the room where he was bidin. And he workit all day, he cam in and had his supper, and he sat and cracked tae the farmer's wife fir a long time till it became bedtime again, till the woman went upstairs tae go tae her bed. And Jack got up again. He got a wee bag and gathered all the pennies, halpenies or whatever kind o' coins they were, and he put them in this wee bag. And he gaes oot wonst again to the graveyard.

There the hoolets were roarin, the moon was comin up and the clouds were passin by. And he waits. Then the auld clock in the steeple o' the church chimes twelve o'clock. Jack dons wonst again the steel plate on his breist, the white sheet ower his shouders, and on wi his glove. In the other hand he held his wee bag o' coins. Up he goes. This time he cam a bit closer to the gate of the auld tomb, which was covered i' ivy, ye could barely see it. And the wind was whistlin, the hoolets were roarin! Which would scare the life o' any human being—but no Jack! He wasnae feart! So he waited and waited. Twelve o'clock cam again. He heard the skreek o' the tomb door openin wonst again. And oot comes the farmer wonst again!

'You're here again,' he says.

'Aye,' says Jack, 'I'm here again. I couldna rest.'

'Why could ye no rest?'

'I've got to come and coont my money!' says Jack. 'I've got to come and coont my fortune. Ye ken, I've got a great fortune, you see!'

'Are ye sure ye're ane o' hus?'

Jack said, 'Of course I'm ane o' youse!'

'Whaur are ye buried? Whaur's yir hole?'

Jack said, 'Come wi me!' And he led him, ower through the graveyard, ower tae where he dug the new fresh grave. He says, 'That's my hole! Dae ye no see the sand whaur I noo cam oot?'

'Well if ye're ane o hus, I felt yir hand last night. Let me feel yir chest tae make sure ye're real—ye're really ane o' hus!'

And Jack pulled back the white sheet fae his chest, and the old farmer put his hand up on Jack's chest. And he feelt the cauld plate. 'Oh, ye're really ane o' hus, ye're really ane o' hus! Seein ye're really ane o' hus,' he says, 'and ye're gaun tae coont yir money, come, and ye come wi me! Because I'm gaun tae coont mine! Follae me!'

And Jack's off after the auld farmer's ghost, up the side o' the wood, up tae a corner of an old dyke, roon the side o' a wee hill tae a wee secret kind o' thing, like a wee den covered in brush and trees. And the old farmer got down on his hands and knees, and Jack crawled after him, with the rattle o' the glove and the rattle o' the plate! And intae a corner among bushes was a big tin box, steel box. And the farmer pulled off the lid of the box. He's flingin handfu's o' gold sovereigns!

He said, 'You think you've got a fortune! Look at this! This is mine, this is mine! Show me yours!'

And Jack said, 'Can I put mine in wi yours?'

'No,' said the old farmer, 'nobody puts nae money in wi mine. This is all mine! And I'll be here every night, and I like playin wi money!'

'Well,' says Jack, 'you play with yours and I'll play wi mine!'

And the old farmer says, 'We dinnae hae much time, it'll soon be one o'clock. I'll have to go back.' And Jack scattered his wee taste o' coins in the grass. And he's lookin for them through the grass and pickin them up and flingin them up in the air. And the old farmer's sittin beside his box o' gold sovereigns, he's flingin them up and playin wi them. Then he closed the lid. 'It's time to go back,' said the old farmer.

Jack said, 'Aye, I think it's time I should go back to my grave tae!' So he said good-bye to the old farmer, watched the old farmer gaun in through the gate to the graveyard. He heard the click o' the door o' the tomb. The old farmer was gone.

Jack hurried back tae his bedroom. Off wi the steel plate, aff with the white sheet, aff with the glove. Rolled them in a knot, flung it in the corner. He had discovered the farmer's secret. He knew, he had marked it well. So when the moon cam up, up goes Jack, back to where he went, up the wee corner, roon the wee corner tae the dyke tae the wee den where the farmer showed him, into the corner where naebody'd ever think! And there hidden in the wee corner where the farmer had sat playin wi his coins was a large tin box. Thousands o' gold sovereigns! Jack carried the whole lot doon wi him. Right doon and put it in his room. He went to his bed.

Next morning after breakfast he says to the farmer's wife,

'Have you got an iron bath, a tin bath, ony kind o' big bath?'

'Ah,' she says, 'there's a big bath in there, but I never use it since my man dee'd. He used tae use it, no me. It's an old iron, an old tin bath.'

He said, 'Could I get it?'

'Oh,' she said, 'what are ye gaunna dae wi it, ye gaunna hae a bath?'

'No,' says Jack, 'I'm no gaunna hae a bath. And I need tae borrow a pail fae ye.' He says, 'Do you hae the key o' yir man's tomb?'

'Oh,' she says, 'Jack, aye, I've got the key. I was the last body to lock the door. But what do ye want it for?'

'Well,' Jack said, 'I've never seen a tomb in my life.'

'But,' she says, 'the're naething in it. It's only a floor and two-three coffins intae it lyin on slabs.'

'Well,' he says, 'look, I would like to have a look at it.'

'Well,' she says, 'my man's ane is the first ane near the door. The other three is his grandfather and granny and all the yins in the tomb.'

'Ah,' Jack said, 'I would just like tae hae a wee look at it.' So she gied Jack the big iron key. Jack got the bath on his shoulder, the iron bath. The farmer's wife went to busy hersel aboot the hoose. She didna ken what Jack was daein.

So Jack goes doon, big iron key on an iron chain. ('Course ghosts dinnae need keys!) Jack, ower to the door, put the key in the old rusty lock, opened it up, creek, pushed the door aside. Walked into a dusty room, covered wi cobwebs. And there were coffins all in a row lyin across. But Jack saw the newest ane. And he dragged it ower close to the waa, away frae the other coffins, on the other side—placed it close up against the waa! Then back he goes and he gets the iron bath. He puts the iron bath 'lang beside in front of it. And he goes for a pail. He fills the bath full o' crystal clear water frae the draw well langsides the coffin! Shuts the

159

door again, locks the door. Goes to the shed o' the wee hoose and gets a wee hammer and a chisel. And he climbs up the top o' the tomb. Right above the bath he drills a nice wide hole that nobody would notice. The reason for Jack drivin the hole on the top o' the tomb—because, just in case the bath ever got empty or the water dried up inside the tomb, every time it rained the water would come through the roof and keep the bath full! Because Jack knew that ghosts and spirits cannae cross clear water. And this was his idea—to keep the old farmer a prisoner in his coffin!

So after he did that he went and he buried the breast plate, he buried the sheet and he buried the glove intae a hole and he covered it in. And he went in tae the farmer's wife and he tellt her the whole story. He showed her the chest o' gold coins.

She says, 'Jack, there's all the money in the world here, we'll never need aa the days o wir life! But I'll get some mair, and that'll dae us the rest o' wir life!' So the farmer's wife sellt the farm for a big price.

Jack and the farmer's wife moved off away to another part o' the country. And they got married. They had as much as to keep them all the days of their life. And Jack had four wee laddies and two wee lassies, a happy family! But the happiest part o' the whole life wi Jack was sittin roon the fire tellin the weans a story—how he'd cheated a ghost!

GLOSSARY

aa all
ae one
airts end wits' end
argued and bargued disputed
avaa at all
awfae awfully
ay always
beautifulest beautiful beyond
  comparison
begint began
bene cowl gentleman (cant)
bene hantle gentry (cant)
bene mort lady (cant)
bi by
bing(s) a lot
bingin coming (cant)
bit piece of
brang brought
brochan gruel
brung brought
but and
cam came
ceilidh get-together
chapped tapped
claes clothes
clift cliff
collop piece of pork
couped tipped
crack small talk

cuddy wooden frame for cutting
  sticks on
dae do
dee'd died
dinna(e) do not
disna does not
div do
doldrums in a daze
done did
doot doubt, expect
drop, wee small amount
empy empty
ett ate
faain falling
fand found
fearin very; livelong
forent foreign
freends friends
gae; gaed go; went
gane went
gang go
gaun; gaunna(e) going; going to
gev gave
gie; gied give; gave
gien gave; given
guddle catch fish with the
  hands
gutters mud
haben food

161

hae have
hale whole
haudin holding
hemmed and hawed aggravated each other
hes has
hev have
hit it (emphatic)
hoolet owl
hurl a lift in a wheeled vehicle
hus us (emphatic)
i' in
jan know (cant)
keeked peeped
ken; kent know; knew
kinnel kindle
langsides lengthwise
lea leave
loss lose
messages groceries
mort lady (cant)
nae no; any
naismort mother (cant)
neeps turnips
oxter upper arm
peenie apron
pishmill ant
pit bing shale from a coal pit
puckle little amount of
quod jail (cant)
raiked scraped; scrounged
roon round
rouch rough
's is; are; has
scaldie down-and-out
scrimping making go as far as possible

scrived worked vigorously
seen saw
set sail started off
shanness shameful (cant)
shouder shoulder
sin since
smiddie smithy
smurach thin bottom layer
strips and straps stripes of many colours
taste, wee little amount of
tattie potato
the day today
the'll there will
the morn tomorrow
the nicht tonight
the noo right now
the're there is; there are
thes these
thon that
thrawn thrown
ti till
to for
two-three a few
waikness hunger
wapped wrapped
wean child
weel well
welt blow
wheesht be quiet
whin bush gorse
wir; wirsels our; ourselves
wonst once
worl world
wrastle wrestle
yese you (pl)
yins ones